THE EVIL B.B. CHOW
AND OTHER STORIES

THE EVIL B.B. CHOW

AND OTHER STORIES

BY STEVE ALMOND

ALGONQUIN BOOKS OF CHAPEL HILL
2005

Published by
Algonquin Books of Chapel Hill
Post Office Box 2225
Chapel Hill, North Carolina 27515-2225

a division of
Workman Publishing
708 Broadway
New York, New York 10003

Stories in this collection originally appeared in the following publications: "The Evil B.B. Chow" in *Zoetrope, Best of Zoetrope II;* "The Soul Molecule" in *Tin House;* "Appropriate Sex" in *Playboy;* "I Am as I Am" in *New England Review;* "A Happy Dream" in *Book* magazine; "Lincoln, Arisen" in *Antioch Review;* "The Idea of Michael Jackson's Dick" on Nerve.com; "The Problem of Human Consumption" in *Virginia Quarterly Review* and *Falling Backwards;* "Wired for Life" in *Missouri Review;* "Summer, as in Love" in *Other Voices* and as "Daisy, over Helpless Shirts, Weeps" in *Arena;* "Larsen's Novel" in *Other Voices;* "Skull" on Nerve.com.

"The Soul Molecule" also appeared in *New Stories from the South.*

Library of Congress Cataloging-in-Publication Data
Almond, Steve.
    The Evil B.B. Chow and other stories / Steve Almond—1st ed.
        p. cm.
    Contents: The evil B.B. Chow—The soul molecule—Appropriate sex—I am as I am—A happy dream—Lincoln, arisen—The idea of Michael Jackson's dick—The problem of human consumption—Wired for life—Summer, as in love—Larsen's novel—Skull.
    ISBN-13: 978-1-56512-422-6
    ISBN-10: 1-56512-422-7
    1. United States—Social life and customs—Fiction.   I. Title.
PS3601.L58E95 2005
813'.6—dc22   2004058564

10 9 8 7 6 5 4 3 2 1
First Edition

To Dr. Barbara Almond,
who taught me to love people,
to love words, to love.
I promise to write if I get work, Ma.

CONTENTS

THE EVIL B.B. CHOW
AND OTHER STORIES

THE EVIL B.B. CHOW

ON FRIDAY, A delivery guy comes to my office with roses in a terra-cotta bowl. Everyone is dying of curiosity, which, of course, so am I. It's not that there aren't men who would send me flowers. There just aren't any men right now.

The card says, "Looking forward to meeting you, Maureen —Warm regards, B.B. Chow."

B.B. Chow?

Marco, my Chief Gay Underling, appears on the other side of my desk. He glances at the flowers.

"A friend," I say.

"Does this friend have a name?"

I hand him the card.

Marco runs his fingernail along the rim of the bowl. "Correct me if I'm wrong, but we don't know any B.B. Chows. Do we?"

"No," I say. "I don't believe we do."

"He sounds like the villain in a Bruce Lee picture," Marco decides. "Like, the Evil B.B. Chow." He does this lame little chop-socky sequence that culminates in him banging his shin against my glass coffee table.

I sit there for a puzzled little moment, listening to Marco yelp and watching the sun bling off this ridiculous desk they gave me when I became Creative Director of *Woman's Work*. It's covered with transparencies of young mothers paring ink stamps from potatoes and oven-roasting their own potpourri. There's always some kid close at hand, gazing at the proceedings in that eerie modulated child model fashion. The moms exude a *wholesome yet edgy* energy that's almost (but not quite) lascivious.

Then it hits me: B stands for Brock. Brock Chow. The man my dear aunt Bev has assured me is an *extremely* handsome doctor. Did I make a date with this man? I check my daily calendar. There, in nonphoto blue, are the words "Bev date."

"Wait a sec," Marco says suddenly. "You didn't send yourself these flowers. We're not there yet, are we boss?"

"Be gone," I tell him. "Go forth to spread malicious gossip."

This is what authority has granted me.

B.B. CHOW DOES not mention the flowers. When I thank him, he blushes, says he hopes they weren't too elaborate. He's about my height, five-seven. A couple of inches shorter, given these absurd mules I tromp around in. A slim guy, narrow through the shoulders and hips. He's got these big, trustworthy features and black hair that falls across his brow like a crow's wing. I can't quite tell if I'm attracted to him or not.

We do one of these new Belgian bistros for dinner and it's clear right away that he's not too familiar with the protocol. When the sommelier comes by he gets confused and orders an appetizer. The whole dual-fork scenario spooks him. I seem to be a slob magnet. In most cases it's these guys who came from money and can't find a more productive way to express self-loathing. But there's nothing practiced to B.B.'s dishevelment. He looks genuinely befuddled, sitting there with his napkin jammed into his sweater collar like a bib.

B.B. is unlike most of the guys I end up dating in one other way: he's not a loudmouth. He speaks so softly I have to lean forward to catch what he's saying. It turns out he's a resident, training to become a pediatric surgeon.

"That must be pretty intense," I say.

"I guess. You know, most of the cases aren't that serious. It maybe sounds more dramatic than it is."

B.B. is obviously more comfortable asking questions, so I lead him through the little tap dance of my life: the condo I just bought in the South End, my new job, my fierce and inexplicable crush on Pedro Martinez. I also tell him that I'm divorced. I've learned not to hold that in reserve, because it generally freaks the single guys out. They either relegate me to this suspect category of fallen woman (Hester Prynne, J.Lo) or they assume I was somehow abused, and it's now incumbent upon them to rescue me. I'm not sure which is worse.

"You look pretty young to be divorced," B.B. says.

"I was only married four years," I say.

"What happened?"

I pause for a moment. "It was kind of a complicated situation."

B.B. nods in such a way that he might actually be bowing. "I'm sorry," he says. "That's probably none of my business, huh? I only meant that it must have been a real disappointment."

I'm not sure what to say. We're lodged in one of those moments of intimacy that's come a bit too quick. B.B. peers at me, in an effort to convey that he *understands* my disappointment. I don't feel especially disappointed, though. I was married to a man who couldn't operate a washing machine. I got out. The end. "I'll tell you what," I say, "I could go for some dessert. Something involving chocolate."

I've invited B.B. to a play out in Jamaica Plain, at this collective art space full of collective art space people. My date looks like a total square. He seems to be making people nervous, which I somewhat enjoy. You can see them squirming in their torn batik. B.B. thinks the whole thing is aces. Loves the play, which is a version of *Endgame* done in the soap opera medium. Loves the after party, which is in the condemned loft next door. He asks the cast members all sorts of sweet, dorky questions. (Example: "Did Beckett have all that nudity in the original version?")

What I like about B.B. is this unchecked enthusiasm. It's a relief, frankly, to hang out with someone who plunges through life without the almighty force field of irony.

"I MEAN, HE *asked permission* to kiss me on the cheek. I've been involved with men who don't even ask permission to come in my mouth."

"Tell me about it," Marco says.

The latest crop of candidates for our "Mad About Mom" section lies between us. There's Sharon Stone (and bodyguard) walking little Roan through Piccadilly Circus, Catherine Zeta-Jones looking lumpy and blissed-out with her diaper bag. "Demi Moore is so *over*," Marco says. "Everything she touches is over."

The truth is she looks radiant. They all look radiant, as if they've drifted into this universe for a single incandescent moment, only long enough to be captured on film. This is what we sell our readers, this illusion of you-*can*-have-it-allness. And we're successful precisely because, beyond all the aspirational blather, back in the drab universe of the day to day, you can't have it all. Not if you want sleep.

The phone rings and Marco snatches it. "Maureen Fleming's office. May I ask who's calling? I'm sorry. She's in a meeting. Yes, I'll let her know. No. No. Good-bye." He shrugs. "Do we know a Mr. Bok Choy?"

As gay underlings go, Marco is unacceptably cheeky. But he's also a decent listener when he wants to be, and he's nursed me through the entire history of my recent romantic pratfalls. *Behind-the-Music* Man (who quoted from the program verbatim). The Incredible Rowing Man (he seemed to confuse my body with an oar). The Sperminator (let's just not discuss this one). Marco coins these sobriquets to keep the lineup straight, and I adopt them to remind myself that these men are only temporary decisions, which can be rescinded.

The phone rings again. "She's busy at the moment, Mr. Choy," Marco says.

"Give me that," I tell him. "Try to remember that I rule you."

B.B. sounds flustered. "I thought you were in a meeting."

"It's over," I say, and motion for Marco to scram.

"I just wanted to say what a nice time I had Friday."

"Yeah. It was nice."

"Can I see you again?"

"Sure."

"When?"

"Well," I say. "I'm kind of booked this weekend."

"Yeah, I am too. This weekend, I mean. I didn't mean this weekend or anything. I meant, like . . ." I can hear him breathing, this sort of wounded rasp.

"Are you okay?"

"Yeah," he says. "A little nervous, I guess. Not sure, you know, if you like me."

"I'm still getting to know you."

"Yeah," B.B. says. "Yeah. Right. I'm sorry. No big deal. Maybe next week. I'm pretty busy anyway, you know, at the hospital. Maybe next week." He's speaking too quickly, too loud. It's always been a weakness of mine: I can't stand to see others in pain. You want an executive summary of the last two years of my marriage? *Ta-da*.

"Wait a sec," I say. "What about an early dinner on Sunday?"

SO THERE I AM, at the Au Bon Pain in Cambridge, on Sunday at five, face-to-face with a focaccia that looks like a giant, cancerous crouton. B.B. is wearing a Harvard Medical School polo shirt, his skinny arms poking out, the same shirt he wore under his sweater last time. It strikes me as odd that this eager beaver is wearing the same shirt. (I know he went to Harvard.) So I sort of make a joke.

"Hey, I've seen that shirt somewhere before."

B.B. looks like I just punched him in the mouth. "Sorry," he says. "These shirts come from the vending machines in the lobby. Sometimes, when you've been on the same rotation for a while, you need a fresh shirt."

And now I see the situation: he's come straight from the hospital, probably left right in the middle of his shift, which would explain why his fingers are stained the color of earwax (Betadine), why he looks frazzled and drawn, why he keeps glancing at his pager.

"You shouldn't be apologizing," I say. "I'm the one who was just an asshole."

"I must look like shit," he says.

"You don't look like shit."

He plucks at his shirt and forces out a laugh. "You should see my closet."

"Look," I say, "you didn't have to cut out on work to see me."

"I wanted to," B.B. says.

There's his face, propped up on his palms like an eager little display.

"I'm flattered," I say. "But there are other times. I mean, I'm not going anywhere."

B.B. takes a deep breath. "I should chill out a little, huh?"

"Maybe a little," I say, and smile. "Hey, I've got a question. What's the second B stand for?"

"Blaine," he says.

"Brock Blaine Chow?"

"Yeah, you know, that was my parents. They wanted to find these super-American-sounding names. The Brock part comes from Lou Brock. My dad was a baseball fan. That was his big thing, you know, the American pastime."

"What about Blaine?"

"Yeah, I think the idea there was Paine. Like Thomas Paine. Give me liberty and all. That was kind of a spelling error."

And now for some reason this annoying little Post-it comes tearing out of my wonkbrain and it says: *Common Sense*. Thomas Paine wrote *Common Sense*. Patrick Henry is the guy who said, "Give me liberty or give me death." But I'm not about to correct B.B., because he's already blushing so fiercely his cheeks are maroon.

"Would you like to get an ice cream?" he asks.

I know I should be scooting along. I've got my own rounds to make, the event schedule I keep overbooked to stamp out any late-weekend embers of anguish. And here's this guy who's obviously, at the very least, neurotic. At the same time, I'm touched by his candor, his overwrought confessions.

It's the first day of spring and the streets finally smell again: tar and garbage, sesame oil, a sweet old perfume. Everywhere, the righteous folk of Cambridge are strolling the polleny avenues, letting the breeze sift their hair. Not even the punks around the T can muster a decent rage, just bits of loud theater, and Harvard Yard seems almost bearable in this mood, rid of its suicide. Students are draped across one another, unbearably young, auditioning for sex in chunky shoes. "B.B." I say, taking his arm, "I like you."

B.B. COMES OVER to my place for the next date. I've decided to revive an old recipe (baked salmon with crumbled gorgonzola, on a bed of orzo) and sconced the lights with colored paper and done all the other inane shit my own magazine recommends in its "Kindling the Flame" column. B.B. buzzes and all I can think is: I hope he doesn't wear the same shirt.

He's wearing the same shirt.

He's also wearing surgical pajamas and paper slippers and carrying a medical bag. In he breezes, calm as you please, kisses me on the cheek, says he's sorry he's late, asks if he can use the bathroom. I'm thinking: enough already. What is this guy's *deal*?

B.B. emerges five minutes later in a full tuxedo. With tails. There are some men who can't carry off a tux. My ex, for instance, always looked hopelessly overmatched, tugging at his cummerbund like an itchy kid. But B.B. looks smashing. His hair is slicked back. His pleats are razors. The black lapels sharpen his features.

We finish off the second bottle of wine and sort of stumble to the couch and now we're really quite close and his skin smells like plums and clay and his eyelashes are so delicate—I've never seen eyelashes so delicate—and I can feel my face get warm and fuzzy as his lips come toward mine.

Sadly, B.B. is not much of a kisser. He presses too hard, and he doesn't know how to modulate the whole mouth-opening-tongue-moving-forward thing. All effort and no technique, which is a marked difference from the guys I usually date, who generally seem to be auditioning for the well-hung/feckless love interest on *Sex and the City*. And yet, I can't help being flattered by his bungling persistence. If push came to shove, I could hog-tie B.B. Chow (I've got at least ten pounds on him). But there he is, groping away at my culottes, smashing his mouth against my bra-cup, whispering, *"You're so sexy, how can you be so sexy?"*

It's gotten late by this time, or early, and I already know I'm going to be a wreck tomorrow, that my gay underlings will watch me in their strange, protective, perversely unjealous manner and fret amongst themselves.

"We should probably call it a night," I say.

B.B. checks his watch. "I've got to be at the hospital in a couple of hours," he says. "Maybe I could just stay here."

"That's not such a good idea."

B.B. leans forward and looks directly into my eyes. "I

want my body next to yours. We can just sleep, but I want to be next to your body. You have such a beautiful body." He's managed to control his voice, but his legs are trembling. It's excruciating. Like watching Oliver Twist ask for more porridge.

"You can stay on the couch," I say. "I'll fix you a place."

"OH SPARE ME," Marco says. "*Spare* me."

"I don't have time for this." I clap my hands unconvincingly. "Go fetch me Evian."

But Marco just sits there, rolling a gummy bear between his fingers. He's not going anywhere until he's secured a full admission.

Which of course he does, how B.B. managed to prolong negotiations, how I managed to relent, blouse by bra by panties, my outfit wrung into colored bulbs on the floor, knowing I shouldn't, knowing the sort of message it sends, but also somewhat relishing throwing off the shackle, ceding to the reckless volition of my sexual adulthood, the old drama of desire stirred against self-protection.

"What's his dick like?" Marco says.

"Stop it," I say. "Don't ask me that kind of shit."

"It's small, isn't it? How small? Uncooked hot-dog small?"

"What it is, the thing that really freaked me out, he's got no hair on his body. Not even under his arms. Just this smooth little, like, pelt. And he doesn't know how to caress. I thought, you know, he's a surgeon. He'll have these delicate fingers. But he's more of a groper. Like being groped by a twelve-year-old."

Marco makes a despicable yum-yum noise.

There's a note on my desk informing me that Phil, the publisher, wants to meet at four to grill me about the Summer of Fun issue ("Not fun enough!"), our new sex columnist ("She looks like a terrier!"), and *occasions for synergy*, a phrase he acquired recently and now chants through the long cappuccino afternoons. When he's done with me, he'll shtup his personal assistant, Mandy, perhaps in his actual office.

Here's what has me baffled: the sex was good. I can't quite explain this to Marco. But somehow, the fact that B.B. Chow can't really kiss or fuck or even fondle, the fact that he makes me feel like Xena, Warrior Princess, these things *turn me on*. It's like the bar is set so low with this guy, we can't help but get over. Which we do. We get over. Twice. Despite all the flubs, the sighing misfires, what comes through is how enraptured the guy is, enraptured by *me*.

And how, just before he left in the morning, stripped of his tux, back in medical scrubs and swaying in the door frame like a eucalyptus leaf, he says this thing to me: "Will you be my girlfriend?" without a lick of irony—with, instead, a look of utmost and moist vulnerability, as if his life depended on the answer.

I don't know what to say. I mean, we've spent the night together, had sex, orgasmed more or less simultaneously. What does that make us? Steadies? I'm not saying I don't understand what he's asking for. It's just such a weird feeling to be on the receiving end of this kind of need. I feel like I should be able to turn to some impartial referee and say, *Flag him, flag him, that's gender preemption!*

WE'VE BOTH GOT these intense schedules. But somehow, rather than slowing the tempo, everything speeds up, launches us into that delirious, two-gear existence, work to bed, bed to work, the narrowing of the social field, the cultivation of baby talk, the entire goopy works. B.B. calls me from the hospital to tell me how much he misses me. He ends every conversation with the same question: "When can I see you?"

This is not to say that I don't have my moments of doubt. The first time I visit B.B. at his apartment, for instance, I spot a photo on his bookcase. A petite blonde, her hair gathered into a ponytail where the roots turn dark. She's wearing a leotard top and cradling a white puppy in her arms.

"Who's this pretty lady?" I call out.

B.B. comes rushing out of the kitchen with a bottle of

wine in one hand and a corkscrew in the other. He sees me examining the photo and looks stricken. "That was a mistake. I apologize." He marches right over and shoves the photo behind his bound copy of *Prenatal Renal Failure*.

"You don't have to do that," I say. "That woman is a part of your life."

"Not anymore. She's my ex."

"Okay. She's your ex," I say. "Does that mean you're not allowed to tell me anything about her?"

"She was an awful cook."

"Where does she live?"

"I don't know," he says brusquely. "Prince Street, I think."

"In the North End? That's right near my friend Marco. He's on Salem."

B.B. shakes his head vehemently. "She means nothing to me. Nothing. You're my girlfriend now." He drops the corkscrew, backs me against the bookshelf, and puts this big clinch on me. The whole thing feels so . . . *staged*. As if I'm playing the role of B.B. Chow's New Girlfriend and he needs scenes like this to keep the action rolling.

"It's like a vortex. I've been sucked into the B.B. Chow Vortex."

"How does he make you feel?" Marco says. He's camped on my love seat, disemboweling a turkey wrap.

"Great," I say. "Horny. Desirous. He notices my shoes. He tells me my feet are beautiful. I mean, you've seen my feet."

"The admission of desire always entails a larger wish," Marco says.

"Who the hell are you, Kung Fu? Quit being so goddamn wise." He's right, of course. My body has started yearning dumbly for permanence. My cheeks are hot all the time and I've stopped obsessing over the skin around my eyes. I feel like the heroine of one of our features: "How I Fell for the Doc Next Door." But it's not just the hormones with B.B. There's something else at play, the terrifying possibility—after years of betting on dumb sexy long shots of the heart, half-knowing how the ride will end—that I've finally found the guy who will love me back. It's enough to send my thighs into rapture.

"Don't tell me how I feel, okay? Tell me what to do."

"What do you want to do?"

"I want to be able to trust this guy," I say quietly.

Marco drops his slice of turkey and looks at me for a long moment. "Maybe you can't handle this guy because he's able to take care of you."

WE'VE BEEN TOGETHER for a month now and for the first time, on a muggy Friday night, something is wrong. B.B. says the right things, but without conviction. He's just present enough to avoid a direct confrontation. But the slow poison of distance hangs around us. When we get back to my place, he climbs onto my bed without undressing.

I lie down next to him. "What's wrong?"

"Nothing."

I place my mouth very close to his ear. "Either you talk about what's going on," I murmur, "or get the hell out of my bed."

B.B. takes a deep breath. "There's this girl," he says.

The back of my neck bristles. "What girl?"

"Last night," he says quickly. "At the hospital." B.B. stares at the ceiling and sighs. "She had what we call craniosynostosis. The sagittal suture fuses too early and the fetal brain distorts the calvarium into an aberrant shape."

"English," I say. I'm looking at B.B. in profile, the black sheen of his eyes, the wet budding of his lips.

"There's no room for the brain," he says. "It grows in the wrong direction, you know. But there's this surgery. To correct the situation."

"What happened?"

"The chief of the unit, you know, he performed the operation. Dr. Balk. He let me assist. It was going fine. You know, they have to cut the cranium and fuse the bone. Then all of sudden her vitals started to drop, you know, the vitals . . ." His voice does a little choked thing. "The respirator, something, there was something wrong. Balk was busy trying to reshape this girl's skull, threading the bone mulch. Her skull, you know, she looked great. But her numbers kept dropping. It wasn't the blood; they gave her another unit of blood. Once the bone is cut, you know, there's no way to control blood loss through the marrow."

The smell of B.B. is suddenly overpowering: a rind of surgical soap soured by sweat. In the park across from my place, the skate rats have gathered under the willows to tell lies. I can hear them spitting at one another and laughing. Farther north, on Tremont, jazz is reeling out from the cafés.

"She looked fine, you know, but she wasn't, like, strong enough. It's what we call operative failure. The heart gives up." His chest starts to heave and I wrap myself around him, pull his head to my bosom, run my fingers through his thatched hair, in the half light of my bedroom, this awkward healer of children with his soft soft lashes, his big broken cheeks. "I'm sorry," he sobs. "I'm so sorry." And now I can feel myself throwing the last anchor of discretion overboard, giving in to the pleasure of giving in, of tending to his tears, his hurt, his deep want of love.

And it's more than this really. I can see now that B.B. is as devastated by this loss as by our ardent duet, that what he's offering me, what his tears offer, is the deepest measure of love: unfettered access to his emotions.

He moves as if injured the next day, though we manage to have a good time, puttering around in pajamas, watching cooking shows, collecting ourselves for some goofy Sadie Hawkins soiree in Somerville. We take the T over, what the hell, watch dusk firing up the Charles, unfolding hopeful pink panels onto the gray rooftops. B.B. is wearing this suede jacket I bought him; I even took the sleeves up an inch with the sewing machine I thought I'd never use again. He looks so adorable that I spend most of the night checking him out from across the room, thinking about his smooth little butt, only half-tuned to the sad angry buzz of gossip that rises from the party with the cigarette smoke.

Later, in the quiet of my bedroom, we make love, and again when the dawn breaks, a languorous morning session. B.B. runs out to get some fresh juice and comes back with flamboyans and snapdragons.

PHIL THE PUBLISHER comes bouncing into my office in his dreadful linen suit, full of dumb suggestions. He makes authoritative hand gestures while I pretend to jot notes. This is our Monday morning ritual. He nods at the stack of proofs on my desk. "Did you come in yesterday?"

"No," I say. "Did you?" What I actually want to say is: "Uh, Phil, why do you smell like pussy? Have you been porking your assistant again?" But the whole situation is just too pathetic.

He finally leaves and I start thumbing through the glossies. What I'm actually doing is trying to remember what it meant to give a shit about all this: the grinning semifamous with their hairdos and rescuing platitudes, the sweet, standing water of self-help. The phone rings and rings. Marco is out sick.

I finally punch up the line.

"Hey," B.B. says.

I can hear the hospital bustle in the background and I picture him cradling the phone in the crook of his neck—his long, smooth neck—and smile. "Hey loverboy."

Silence.

"Are you okay?" I say.

B.B. says something, but so softly I can't quite hear him.

"What is it, honey?"

"I can't do this," he says.

"Do what?"

"I'm still in love with Dinah," he says quickly. "It's not fair for us to spend any more time. Not fair to you."

"Wait a second," I say. "What are you talking about?"

"I'm still in love with Dinah."

"*What?*"

B.B. starts crying.

I feel, in my chest, the slapping of wings around a dark emptiness. Then the endorphins come roaring in and my heart does the little two-step into rage. "Why are you telling me this on the phone? Why am I hearing this from a goddamn piece of plastic?"

"I'm sorry," B.B. sobs.

"You've got to be kidding." I slam the phone down.

The lesser gay underlings, sensing a disturbance in the Boss Force, have clumped outside my office. In Marco's absence, one of them will soon be nominated to check in on me. I regulate my breathing and call B.B. back. He comes to the phone in tears.

"Stop that," I say. "Be a man, for crying out loud. Be a man and tell me how long you've known this."

"A couple of days," he whispers.

"So you knew on Saturday, when I gave you that jacket? And you knew at the party. And you knew when you fucked me Saturday night, and Sunday morning. And when you brought me those fucking flowers? You knew. But you didn't have the guts to tell me, is that your testimony, you little piece of shit?"

B.B. blows his nose. "I was trying to make sure, you know, I wanted you to have a great weekend. I felt I owed you that."

And here I find myself, in my ripening thirtyish cynicism, newly confounded by the perversity of male logic. Best to dump someone on a high note? Is this the way men think? As if love were a discrete property, something one accrues, like money or promotions? But surely B.B. is empathic enough to recognize I had gone into full meltdown. And this must have made him panic. He's one of those men who conducts his love life like a catch-and-release program. Though it's worse than that actually, because B.B. made me feel safe by showing me *his* insecurity. While my ex, for instance, played himself in public as a seducer and a tough, then wound up privately clinging to me for years. Which just goes to show how little women can know of their men—because men know so little of themselves.

Or maybe this is just the line they run. Maybe they know what they're doing the whole time. They'll give you an office and a desk and a title. But, in the end men win, always, because they can better withstand their own poor behavior.

B.B. is saying something, sniveling about what a fool he is, as if even at this point we might collaborate in a final scene, commemorating his guilt. I want to shout: *I was going to teach you how to kiss! You can't do this!* But giving him anything else, a single word, seems absurd.

I call Marco at home and the machine picks up. The glossies are staring at me, tireless and beatific in their gospel of self-improvement, urging me and all the other mes in the bleary sorority of millennial womanhood to find our G-spots, to insist on equal pay, to revamp the drapes and consider a diaper service, to do anything but succumb to our own truest feelings of anger and inadequacy.

I TROMP ACROSS the godforsaken Government Plaza, through the fishy stink of Hay Market and into the North End. I could just barf at the quaintness of it all: the zephyrs of garlic and dusty bricks, the old paisano peddling shaved ice under the weather-stripped cupola. But I need some tea and teary commiseration and I need Marco's bullshit wisdom and I need a hug.

Marco lives on Salem. But the moment I see the sign for Prince Street, I start thinking about Dinah. Dinah who lives on Prince Street. There must be something she possesses that I don't, some emotional or sexual power, some nonthreatening poise. *Something*. Because otherwise he would've chosen me. And now it occurs to me that I have wound up near Prince Street not entirely by chance, that some darker, unraveled part of me is hoping to find and confront Dinah. So that, rather than hurrying on to Salem—surely the prudent course—I find myself sort of hovering on the corner, though what I'm actually doing (it occurs to me unpleasantly) is *skulking,* a verb I had hoped to avoid during my brief tenure on earth.

The old man selling shaved ice smiles at me.

"You want-a eat a good meal?" he says.

"No."

"Good-a calamari."

"No thank you. Really."

He continues to smile at me, suspiciously now, and I flee

onto Prince Street and begin checking the numbers on the apartment houses in a very obvious way, then looking down at an invisible slip of paper in my hand, as if I'm part of the census bureau, a special agent sent out to ask the locals random questions such as: *Is there a skinny little slut living on the premises who might have stolen my Chinese boyfriend?*

I've been at this for anywhere from fifteen minutes to perhaps an hour, when a strange thing happens: a woman strides out of the building across the street with a tiny white dog. She looks just like in the photo: dyed blond hair, leotard top. Her waist is the circumference of a baguette, and she has that ducky dancer walk, mons pubis thrust forward, like a pregnant woman minus the child.

I cross the street and walk up to her: "Can I say hello to your dog?" I'm wearing a tailored suit and pumps—an outfit that favors the irrational gesture.

Dinah shrugs. "Sure."

I bend down. "Hey there. What's your name?"

"Charmie," Dinah says.

"Hey there, Charmie." Then I look up and say, "Hey there, Dinah."

"*He-ey.*" Dinah cocks her head. I can see her rifling through her little change purse of a mind, trying to recall how she might know me.

"You don't know me," I say. "I'm a friend of Brock Chow's. He told me you lived around here."

"Oh."

"Actually. I used to go out with Brock. But he just broke up with me. Just a few minutes ago. He told me he's still in love with you."

Dinah takes a half step backwards; little tremors of dread vine the skin around her mouth. I keep petting her dog. The fur around its eyes is the color of dried blood. A cumulonimbus has drifted over the spires of downtown, where it hangs like a vast gray anvil. I imagine how this would play in the magazine: "Hex His Ex: How to Confront the Woman Who Stole Your Man!" (Maybe a Photoshop illustration of a voodoo doll in a miniskirt?)

"Do you have a few minutes?" Dinah says. "Like, to talk?"

THE MOMENT I step into her apartment, I know I've made a mistake. The decor is what Marco would call Early Porno. Popcorn ceilings. A particle-board entertainment center. There's dust on the sills, crusty dishes in the sink, a to-do list yellowing on the fridge. The air smells sharp and rotten and a dull wet chopping noise comes from down below, a butchering sound.

"Sorry about the smell," Dinah says. "There's, like, the landlord put out some of those poison traps. My roommate's boyfriend said he'd find . . . whatever it is."

"You have a roommate?"

"She only spends about half the time here."

I'm just about to ask Dinah where, precisely, a room-mate would stay, when I notice a door located *behind the stove*.

"Do you want some juice?" Dinah says. "We've got some great juice." She pulls a plastic cup from the cupboard, the kind they give away at baseball games.

"That's okay," I say. "I'm actually supposed to be visiting a friend."

"Yeah," Dinah says. "Anyway, you know, Brock's started calling me again." She gestures, indicating that I should take a seat.

"I sort of figured."

"You have to understand about Brock. He's so, like, in-secure. He'll be with one girl, but then he starts thinking about his last girlfriend. It happened to me, too," she says. "He left me for this girl, Tina." She touches the sleeve of my blouse and her hand lingers there for a moment, as if what she really wants is to play the material between her fingers. "It's not even his fault, really. His parents, you know, they put a lot of pressure on him."

Dinah picks up her dog and traverses the room. She wants me to see how graceful she is, I think. She plops Charmie onto her desk. On the wall behind her is a sam-pler that reads: I'M A DANCIN FOOL, WHAT'S YOUR EXCUSE?

"And it's not like I called him back," she says. "He's a

great guy and all. I think it's amazing what he does. But I've really been trying to do some work on myself, like, inter-personal stuff. And Brock is someone, you know, he can be a little, like, too much."

The phone rings and we both freeze. "I'm going to let the machine pick that up," Dinah announces. Charmie starts darting around the desk. The machine clicks on and Dinah's desperately cheery outgoing message fills the room. Then there's a long beep and we both stand there not look-ing at one another.

Whoever it is hangs up.

"How long were you guys involved, anyway?" Dinah says.

"Not long."

She nods and her ponytail bobs. "Were you guys, like, intimate?"

"Listen," I say. "I should really get going."

"Yeah, I just wanted, you know." Dinah makes a little tossing gesture. "Brock is kind of a confused guy. But he's got a good heart. The work he does, you know, it's really the work of saints. I remember one time, right before we broke up, he came back from the hospital and he was just, you know, wiped out. Because he'd seen this little girl die during an operation. There was something wrong with her skull."

The air seems to thicken around me, and I have to lean

against the door to support myself. "Do you have a bath-room?" I say.

"That's the one thing that's kind of weird about this place," Dinah says. "The bathroom is actually, like, in the hallway."

I stumble out the door and into the bathroom and drop to my knees over the bowl, which is stained with what I hope is rust, and my body begins to clench.

Dinah's outside asking if everything's okay, do I need anything? "I'm okay. Just girl stuff."

"Maybe I could get your number," Dinah says through the door. "In case you want to talk some more."

"Sure," I say. "Just give me a minute." I sag back from the toilet and glance at the milk crate full of magazines under the sink. Right on top is Cher's face, winched by countless surgeries and beaming from the cover of our Survivor's issue, alongside Tina Turner and Oprah. Dinah has every issue of *Woman's Work* dating back three years. She's folded down the corners of certain pages. I feel ready to weep.

DOWN BELOW, ON the orange sidewalks, with their steadying smell of baked yeast, I want to feel vindicated, to know that B.B. dumped me for this wreck, that he's sim-ply one of *those* men. And I want to feel relief, that he wasn't in my life long enough to do much damage. I've been in far worse entanglements, where the shared data was extensive and the smells haunted my clothing for weeks. Most of all I want to feel my rage again, at the world of men, who never tire of exploiting our ability to care, our hardwired weakness for weakness.

I know I should toddle off to Marco's now and have a good cry and listen to his sweet useless pep talk and pretend to make sense of it all. But there's nothing in me but weariness. I'm weary of moving through life in this way, punished for my capabilities, betrayed by the glib promises of love. I'm weary of managing these disappointments. I'm weary of my body's gruesome tick. And I'm weary of telling women it can be different.

Instead, I wander the docks, the old schooners burdened under ornate masts, the colonial cemetery dressed in gravestones, names and years in elegant rows, and roasted garlic everywhere, everywhere tourists in their pink summer legs and dusk on the bricks, rain gutters fat with pigeons and rooftops sprigged with antennae, the sediments of beauty, I mean, and the widows on their stoops, done with the suffering of men and silent before the soft click of bocce balls. There is so much time in this life for grief. So many men lying in wait. And here, tonight, there is a harvest moon, which hangs so heavily yellow above the sea it might be God, or my heart.

THE SOUL MOLECULE

I was on my way to see Wilkes. We were going to have brunch. Wilkes was a minor friend from college. He played number one on the squash team. I'd challenged him once, during a round-robin, and he annihilated me with lobs. Afterwards, in the showers, he told me his secret.

"Vision," he said. "You have to see what's going to happen."

Now it was five years on and I still felt sort of indebted to him. This was idiotic but I couldn't unpersuade myself. I kept remembering those lobs, one after another, as elegant as parasols.

Wilkes was in the back of the restaurant, in a booth. We said our hellos and he picked up his menu and set it down again.

"We've known each other a long time, haven't we, Jim?"

"Sure," I said.

"Eight years now, coming up on eight."

"That sounds about right."

"You wouldn't think less of me if I told you something, would you?"

"Heck no," I said. Mostly, I was wondering how much breakfast would cost, and whether I'd have to pay.

"I've got a cartridge in my head," Wilkes said.

He had that drowsy pinch around the eyes you see in certain leading men. He was wearing a blue blazer with discreet buttons. He looked like the sort of guy from whom other guys would buy bonds. That was his business. He was in bonds.

"A cartridge has been placed in my head for surveillance purposes. This was done a number of years ago by a race of superior beings. I don't know if you know anything about abduction, Jim. Do you know anything about abduction?"

"Wait a second," I said.

"An abduction can take one of two forms. The first— you don't need to know the technical terms—the first is purely for research purposes. Cell harvesting, that kind of thing. The second involves implants, Jim, such as the one in my brain."

Wilkes was from Maryland, the Chesapeake Bay area. He spoke in these crisp, prepared sentences. I'd always thought he'd be a corporate lawyer, with an office in a glass tower and a secretary better-looking than anyone I knew.

"You're telling me you've been abducted," I said.

Wilkes nodded. He picked up his fork and balanced it

on his thumb. "The cartridges can be thought of as visual recorders, something like cameras. They allow the caretakers to monitor human activity without causing alarm."

"The caretakers," I said.

"They see whatever I see." Wilkes gazed at me for a long moment. It was eerie, like staring into the big black space where an audience might be. Finally, he looked up and half rose out of his seat. "Mom," he said. "Dad. Hey, there they are. You remember Jim."

"Why of course," said his mother. She was a southern lady with one of those soft handshakes.

"Pleasure," Mr. Wilkes said. "Unexpected pleasure. No no. Don't make a fuss. We'll just settle in. What are you up to, Jim? How're you bringing in the pesos?"

"Research," I said.

His face brightened. "Research, eh? The research game. What's that, biotech?"

"Yeah, sort of."

I'd never done any research. But I liked the way the word sounded. It sounded broad and scientific and beyond reproach.

"Your folks?" Mr. Wilkes said.

"You'll remember us to them, I hope," Mrs. Wilkes said.

I had no recollection of my parents having met the Wilkeses.

"What are you two bird dogs up to?" Mr. Wilkes said.

He was from Connecticut, but he sometimes enjoyed speaking like a Texan.

Wilkes was squeezed next to his dad and his voice was full of that miserable complicated family shit. "We were talking," he said. "I was telling Jim about the cartridge in my head."

Mr. Wilkes fixed him with a look and I thought for a second of that Goya painting, Saturn wolfing his kids down like chicken fingers. Mrs. Wilkes began fiddling with the salt and pepper, as if she might want to knit with them eventually.

"How about that?" Mr. Wilkes said. "What do you think of that, Jim?"

"Interesting," I said.

"*Interesting*? That the best you can do? Come on now. This is the old cartridge in the head. The old implant-a-roony."

I started to think, right then, about this one class I'd taken sophomore year, the Biology of Religion. The professor was a young guy who was doing research at the medical school. He told us the belief in a higher power was a function of biological desire, a glandular thing. The whole topic got him very worked up.

Mr. Wilkes said: "Do you know why they do it, Jim?"

"Sir?"

He turned to his son again. "Did you explain the integration phases to him? The hybrids? The grays? Anything?"

"He just got here," Wilkes said.

Mr. Wilkes was sitting across from me. He was one of these big Republicans you sometimes see. The gin blossoms, the blue blazer. His whole aura screamed: *yacht*.

"They teach you any folklore in that fancy college of yours? Fairy, dybbuk, goblin, sprite. Ring a bell, Jim? These are the names the ancients used to describe our extraterrestrial caretakers. *Their appearance was like burning coals of fire and like the appearance of lamps: it went up and down among the living creatures, and the fire was bright and out of the fire went forth lightning*. That's straight from the Book of Ezekiel. What's that sound like to you, son? Does that sound like God on his throne of glory?"

"No," I said. "I guess not."

"There's a reason Uncle Sam launched Project Blue Book," Mr. Wilkes said. "He was forced to, Jim. Without some kind of coherent response, there'd be no way to stem the panic. Let me ask you something. Do you know how many sightings have been reported to the Department of Defense in the past ten years? Guess. Two point five million. Abductions? Seven hundred thousand plus. They are among us, Jim."

Our waitress had appeared.

"Do you serve Egg Beaters?" Mr. Wilkes said.

The waitress shook her head.

"Toast," Mrs. Wilkes said. "You can have some toast, dear."

"I don't want toast," Mr. Wilkes said.

Wilkes looked pretty much entirely miserable.

"What about egg whites," Mr. Wilkes said. "Can you whip me up an omelet with egg whites?"

The waitress shifted her weight from one haunch to the other. She was quite beautiful, though dragged down by circumstance. "An omelet with what?" she said.

"The white part of the egg. The part that isn't the yolk." Mr. Wilkes picked up his fork and began to simulate the act of scrambling eggs.

"I'm asking what you want *in* the omelet, sir."

"Oh. I see. Okay. How about mushroom, swiss, and bacon."

"*Bacon?*" said Mrs. Wilkes.

I didn't know what the hell to order.

The waitress left and Mr. Wilkes turned right back to me. He'd done some fund-raising for the GOP and I could see now just how effective he might be in this capacity. "Mrs. Wilkes and I, we both have implants. It's no secret. Not uncommon for them to tag an entire family. Did Jonathon already explain this?"

"I didn't explain anything," Wilkes said. "You didn't give me a chance."

"Yes," Mrs. Wilkes said. "You musn't dominate the conversation, Warren."

"Remember Briggs?" Wilkes said.

"Who?"

"Briggs. Ron Briggs. Played number four on the team. He's got an implant. He lives out in Sedona now."

"Do we know him?" Mrs. Wilkes said.

Mr. Wilkes waved his hand impatiently. "Now I'm not going to bore you with some long story about our abductions, Jim. How would that be? You show up for breakfast and you have to listen to *that*. What you need to understand is the role these beings play. If they wanted to destroy us, if that was their intent, hell, I wouldn't be talking to you right now. They're caretakers, Jim. An entire race of caretakers. I'm not trying to suggest that these implants are any bed of roses, mind you. You've got all the beta waves to contend with, the ringing. Val's got a hell of a scar."

Mrs. Wilkes blushed. She had an expensive hairstyle and skin that looked a bit irradiated. "He's going to think we're kooks," she said.

"Not at all," I said quietly.

"Hell, we *are* kooks," Mr. Wilkes said. "The whole damn species is kooks. Only a fool would deny it."

I waited for the silence to sort of subside and excused myself. I needed some cold water on my ears. I filled the sink and did a quick dunk and stared at the bathroom mirror—really *stared*—until my face got all big-eyed and desperate.

When I got back to the table, the food had arrived and

the Wilkeses were eating in this extremely polite manner. I'd visited them once, on the way back from a squash match at Penn. All I could remember about their home was the carpets. They must have had about a thousand of them, beautiful and severe, the kind you didn't even want to step on. I couldn't imagine a kid growing up in that place.

My French toast was sitting there, with some strawberries, but I wasn't hungry.

Mrs. Wilkes frowned. "Is something wrong with your food, dear? We can order you something else."

"That was pretty funny," I said finally. "You guys really had me going. You must be quite the charades family."

The Wilkeses, all of them, looked at me. It was that look you get from any kind of true believer, this mountain of pity sort of wobbling on a pea of doubt.

I thought about my biology professor again. Toward the end of class, just before I dropped out in fact, he gave us a lecture about this one chemical that gets released by the pineal gland. He called it the soul molecule, because it triggered all kinds of mystical thoughts. Just a pinch was enough to have people talking to angels. It was the stuff that squirted out at death, when the spirit is said to rise from the body.

Mr. Wilkes was talking about the binary star system Zeta Reticuli and the Taos Hum and the Oz Effect. But you could tell he wasn't saying what he really wanted to. His face was red with the disappointed blood.

The waitress came and cleared the dishes.

Wilkes started to mention a few mutual friends, guys who made me think of loud cologne and urinals.

Mrs. Wilkes excused herself and returned to the table with fresh makeup.

Mr. Wilkes laid down a fifty. It was one of his rituals and, like all our rituals, it gave him this little window of expansiveness.

"I don't know the exact game plan, Jim. Anyone tells you they do, head the other direction. But I do know that these beings, these grays, they are essentially good. Why else would they travel 37 light-years just to bail our sorry asses out? It's the mission that affects me," he said. "Mrs. Wilkes and Jonathon and I, all of us, we feel a part of something larger." He gazed at his wife and son and smiled with a tremendous vulnerability. "I know how it looks from the outside. But we don't know everything. We all make mistakes." He tried to say something else, but his big schmoozy baritone faltered.

Mrs. Wilkes put her hand on his.

"What the hell do I know?" Mr. Wilkes said.

"We all make mistakes," his wife said.

"I'm not perfect."

"Nobody's perfect, love."

There was a lot passing between them. Wilkes started to blush. His father seemed to want to touch his cheek. "They're just trying to save us from ourselves, so we don't ruin everything."

The waitress had come and gone and left change on the table. All around us people were charging through their mornings, toward God knows what.

The Wilkeses were sitting there, in their nice clothing, but I was seeing something else now, these whitish blobs at the centers of their bodies. It was their spirits I was seeing. I wasn't scared or anything. Everyone's a saint when it comes to the naked spirit. The other stuff just sort of grows over us, like weeds.

I thought about that crazy professor again. He'd called me to his office after Thanksgiving to tell me I was flunking. He was all torn up, as if he'd somehow betrayed me. He asked if I'd learned anything at all in his class. I said of course I had, I'd learned plenty of things, but when he pressed me to name one or two, I drew a blank. Just before I left, he came over to my side of the desk and put his hand on my shoulder and said, *We all need someone to watch over us, James.*

"Do you believe that?" Mr. Wilkes said.

I was pretty sure I'd never see the three of them again and it made me a little sad, a little reluctant to leave.

Wilkes was smoothing down his lapels. Mrs. Wilkes

smiled with her gentle teeth and Mr. Wilkes began softly, invisibly, to weep. His spirit was like a little kerchief tucked into that big blue suit.

"I think we're going to be alright," I said. "That's the feeling I get." This was true. I was, in fact, having some kind of clairvoyant moment. Everything that was about to happen I could see, just before it did.

Outside, up in the sky, above even the murmuring satellites, an entire race of benevolent yayas was maybe peering down at me with glassy black eyes. I started waving. The waitress breezed by and blew me a kiss. Mr. Wilkes slid another fifty across the table and winked. The sun lanced through a bank of clouds and lit the passing traffic like tinsel. I waved like hell.

APPROPRIATE SEX

THIS WAS A FRIDAY in April, one of the last days of the term, and the undergrads were all worked up. You could see it in the way they touched themselves, those lewd innocent little caresses of the self, the way they lingered over their cigarettes out on the steps, a thousand bright sucking lips.

The dress code in my own class was terrifying. Cutoffs. Halter tops. Garments that managed to fuse the sartorial aspirations of sportswear and lingerie. Spring was finally here (finally! finally!) and there was no holding the young skin back.

We were critiquing a story called "Last Rites," in which a mother mourning the death of her daughter decides, rather impulsively, to visit the girl's prize Arabian stallion.

"What's the deal with the horse?" said Brendan Mahoney. "Is there something, like, *going on* with the horse?"

"What would be going on with the horse?" said Nicole Buswell.

Nicole—pale, chubby, ardently sexless—was our leader

for the day. I myself didn't lead discussions. I felt this would inhibit the class, and my philosophy as a teacher back then was to disinhibit.

"I don't know," Brendan said. "I'm not saying anything, like, explicit, but—" He looked down at his copy of the story and squinted. "There's this line at the top of seven: 'She felt the heat of the animal against her body. The animal heat entering her.' What's that mean: 'The animal heat entering her'?"

There was a pause.

"Oh, that's sick," said Emily Givens.

"She goes and leans against the horse," said Rob Tway. "It's a human thing. Like wanting, like, contact. She's just decided to take her daughter off life support."

"That's what makes the whole thing so weird!" Brendan said, as if Rob had helped him make his point. "I mean, if she's so upset about her daughter and all, what's she doing getting all sexualized over a horse?"

"Sexualized?" said Nicole. "Sexualized isn't even a *word*."

"Yes it is," said Pete Fayne.

"All that stuff about the thick neck and the satiny hair or whatever," Brendan said. "It's like she's gonna hump the horse or something."

"Sick," said Emily Givens. "You are *so* sick."

I had the feeling, actually, that Emily knew a little something about sick. She was wearing a top that would have

44

been illegal in key southern states, a kind of cheesecloth camisole.

"You're really twisted," said Rob Tway, and Nick Hutchins chipped in, "Uncalled for, dude. Majorly."

Brendan shook his head. He was the lowest common denominator, no doubt about that, a dim kid with the long, rutted cheeks of adolescence. But he was only following my lead. I was the one who had ordered them to root out the truth, to never avert their eyes. *Self-deception,* I'd told them, in my profound deeply feeling teacher voice, *is the only worthy enemy.*

"I'm just saying," Brendan said. "Like, look at it. 'She stroked the beast's hot, damp, thick, satiny neck. She smelled the musk of the animal enveloping her trembling body.' I didn't write that. Did I write that?"

He looked at me.

"You did not write that," I said.

Nicole let out a puff of disgusted air.

The author, Mandy Shaw, sat scribbling in her notebook. She was a sadistic little sex bomb with a tattoo on the small of her back of a fairy princess with blue hair and D cups. Sometimes, during conferences, as she sat across from me fretting over syntax, I imagined her body rendered on black velvet. The faintest hint of her body spray was enough to ruin my day.

"Even the way the daughter is described. The way she

rides the horse, like the way their bodies fit together. And the mom's watching, remembering how her daughter's face looked." Brendan started flipping through the story again.

"Let's move on," Nicole said.

"Hold on, hold on. Here it is. 'The look on Cassie's face was one of unbridled ecstasy, as if her body were rising on some large, warm happiness.' Am I crazy or does that sound kind of horny? Come on. Large. *Warm*." Brendan looked for support to Teddy Leaf, his fellow burnout. "I'm not saying the mom doesn't love Cassie or isn't heartbroken or whatever. It's just there's all this weird, like, energy with the horses. Like this sexy horse energy."

This drew a few laughs and Brendan began to nod. "We all know about those girls, those horsey girls, who are all obsessed with horses. Going out to the barn and brushing them and washing their flanks and all that. Rubbing them down. Marie-Antoinette—she had sex with horses."

"That was Catherine the Great, you idiot," said Rob Tway.

"They had to use a crane to lower the animal down onto her," Pete Fayne added helpfully.

"Please don't call him an idiot," I said to Rob.

"Who did?" said Teddy Leaf.

"Her attendants," said Fayne. "The dudes who help out the queen."

Teddy Leaf ran a finger over the scab on his elbow.

"That's, like, treason dude. Watching the queen fuck a horse is definitely treason."

"Why are we talking about this?" Nicole said.

"Brendan's just making stuff up to get attention because his parents didn't give him enough when he was a child," said Emily Givens.

"I didn't make that up," Brendan said. "It's history."

"Gross," Emily said. "You are *made* of gross."

"You'd know," said Teddy Leaf, and the class, the entire little circle of creative fucknuts, let out a lowdown murmur.

All except for Ingrid Nunez. She was a strict Pentecostal who wrote stories about her love for the All-Knowing Creator of Man and, more recently, her devout hope that the iniquitous would burn in hell for the rest of time.

"I do think we're getting a little far afield," I said.

They'd stuffed us in the basement of Krass, in an airless little cell that smelled of chicken nuggets, which Teddy Leaf brought to class each week, despite my repeated implorations. I gazed out the window, at the parking lot with the Dumpsters. The nice classrooms, the ones with natural light and a view of the courtyard's lush flower beds, were reserved for the business school, where it was assumed the students might someday become prosperous.

"Wait a second," Brendan said. "What's so gross? Why are you guys all, like, ganging up on me? I'm just talking about what Mandy wrote in her story. I'm not trying to offend her. Mandy, I'm not trying to offend you. I liked the story. I wrote, like, a whole critique."

Brendan Mahoney was not a promising student. He was the sort of student whose intellectual life might have been titled *Still Life with Bong*. But now, on this gorgeous April day, the wick of insight had been lit within him and he came at us with the force of a crusader. He knew he was right, that he'd latched onto a little node of perversion below the story's maudlin surface, and he wasn't going to let it go.

"Sex and death are related," he explained. "The French, the French people, when they come, they call that dying. Sex dying."

"A little death," said Rob Tway.

"Right," Brendan said. "The point being that both of those things, like, dying, like when you die, and when you have sex, they're like the same thing in a certain way."

"A dead fuck," Teddy Leaf said.

"So like this mom, when she goes out to visit the horse, she's trying to connect to her daughter, right? But when she thinks about her daughter she thinks about how she used to ride the horse and how her daughter used to be, like, all *excited* to ride the horse. And as she's describing this, that's when she starts touching the horse, like rubbing it all over and getting all this heat entering her body and so forth."

Nicole Buswell was glaring at me now, with her sharp

white teeth, and Emily Givens had bugged out her eyes. Rob Tway said, "You don't have any idea what Mandy had in her mind when she wrote the story—"

"Yeah, but you can write something and not even know what it's about until you, like, look at it later and figure it out. Isn't that right, Mr. Lowe? That's even got a name."

"Perversion in the service of the ego," Emily Givens said.

"I'm not trying to be a pervert," Brendan said.

"You don't *have* to try," Emily said.

It occurred to me suddenly that these two had fucked and that it had ended badly, as it usually does at that age, and that this probably explained the extra erotic charge I'd sensed in class over the past few weeks.

There were other factors. I should mention, for instance, that all this took place during the Lewinsky scandal, and as much as I hate to invoke that dark episode, it is relevant, because everyone back then, including the *New York Times* and the United States Congress was talking about blow jobs, was imagining President Clinton with his pants around his ankles and his naked Presidential ass pressed against his Presidential desk and his Presidential face all cragged up in bliss and Monica on her knees wrapping her big red mouth around his pecker. The Altoids hummer. The Cohiba up her snatch. The money shot onto the blue dress. This was our political discourse.

And what's more, it was everything we'd ever wished for,

to see our big daddy Prez getting down with some chubby hayseed in the Oral Office. It was what we deserved. Our popular culture had prepared us exquisitely for the whole shebang. Practically everywhere you turned, strangers were preparing to have sex, or talking about sex, advising us on how to lick a woman's private parts.

I was one of the only adults who wasn't having sex at that historical moment, because my wife had left me, though actually, we hadn't had sex for a year or so before that because I had lost my desire for her and could not maintain an erection and while I had learned to compensate in various ways my wife had put two and two together and decided I was having an affair with one of my students, which, oddly, I was not.

Brendan was still pleading his case. He had taken off his visor so that he could wave it around a little, and this had exposed a vibrant white band of skull. He looked—in his cargo pants and high-tops—like a vehement hip-hop mushroom.

"Terrific," I said. "You've made some cogent points, Brendan. Let's hear from someone who hasn't had a chance yet." My glance settled, rather unfortunately, onto Ingrid Nunez. She was biting her lower lip.

"What do you think, Ingrid?"

"Brendan is going to burn in hell for the rest of time," she said quietly.

"That seems a little severe," I said.

"What about Mandy?" Nicole Buswell said. "She's supposed to be able to ask questions at the end, Mr. Lowe."

"Of course," I said. "Any questions?"

Mandy was wearing the sort of lip gloss that made her look like she'd just gone ten rounds with a stick of butter. She'd settled on a conservative outfit for the day, which meant you had to imagine what her nipples looked like, using only texture as a guide. She looked down at her notebook and back up at me and licked her lips and smiled and began to run her bracelets up and down her wrist. There was nothing I could do about any of this. They hadn't come up with those kinds of arrest warrants yet.

"Nope," she said. "None."

This meant it was time for class to be over, which meant—given that I could no longer tolerate being on campus for more than one afternoon a week—that it was time for office hours.

No one ever came to office hours except Rob Tway, who had always read something life altering and wanted to discuss its narrative arc and authorial stance and other *issues of craft* which I managed to avoid because I didn't really understand what craft was, frankly, and because I no longer read anything written after the Civil War. I endured these onslaughts only by reminding myself that someday Rob Tway would commit suicide.

"What are we going to do about this Mahoney?" Tway said. "It's probably too late to put him on academic probation. But we could always ask him to withdraw." Tway took out a pack of sugarless gum and whacked it against the heel of his palm. "We've got till April 15."

"I was thinking maybe of just letting it slide. Chalking it up to critical enthusiasm."

"That was harassment, Mr. Lowe. With all due respect."

Tway now launched into a lengthy discourse on *Tristram Shandy,* a book I might have actually read, except that I hadn't.

There was a knock on the door. This was a wondrous thing! A knock. On the door.

"I'll need to see who that is," I said.

Tway checked his watch and frowned.

I opened the door and there stood Mandy Shaw. She had changed into a tank top and what looked like a pair of boxer shorts and her little scent cloud smelled of coconut and cigarettes.

"Hey," she said.

"Hey."

"Are you, like, available?"

"Yes. Of course. Rob was just finishing up."

"No I wasn't," said Tway.

"Yes, you were."

Mandy flounced into my office and suddenly I was mortified by the decor—the antidrug poster clipped from a newspaper and taped to the door, the erotic renderings of Plato and Socrates. These had been put up by my office mate, a gentleman named Jeffrey Thist, whom I had never met and who was, apparently, a classicist in recovery.

I watched Mandy settle into her seat. "How do you think it went in there?" I said.

"In where?"

"In class."

Mandy had bound her hair up with a chopstick and the loose strands kept brushing her cheeks. "How did it *go*?" she said uncertainly.

"The critique of your story."

"I haven't read them yet," she said. "They're in my back-pack."

"Right. I meant the discussion."

"The discussion?"

"Of your story. The discussion of your story in class. I was concerned that some of the comments may have been a little upsetting."

"Which comments?"

"Well, for instance, the comments that Brendan was making."

"Brendan?"

"Brendan Mahoney." I paused. "Those observations he made about the mother in your story." Mandy's legs were crossed and one of her flip-flops was dangling off her toes, which were painted metallic blue. "I worried those might have upset you."

"In what way?"

"Just that Brendan was saying that Susan, the character Susan, that when she thought about her daughter, how much her daughter loved her horse, that there was an erotic element to her, the mother's, thinking."

"Uh-huh."

"Yes?"

"I'm not sure I'm following you," Mandy said.

"Right," I said. "Okay. Remember in class, we were talking about your story and Brendan read those lines about the mom and the horse. And he was suggesting that the mom might have had certain feelings toward her daughter's horse. Feelings of a sexual sort. That she might have had some sexual feelings for the horse. I was worried this might have upset you. Because sometimes, as I've said, we write things and people might take them differently from the way we intended. Brendan was not passing judgment on you, or suggesting that you think about horses in a sexual way."

"But I do," said Mandy Shaw.

She had the face of a doomed starlet—small, round features that expressed a kind of contemptuous yearning. Watching her apply lip gloss made you want to grab God by the lapels and shout: Now, why did you have to go and arrange *that*? My fantasies about her, conjured during failed efforts with the wife, were sad and prosaic. Mandy on a bearskin rug. Mandy with whipped cream. Mandy insisting that I take my lashes like a man.

"Oh my God, I used to think about horses *all the time*," she said. "They're so big and, like, strong, you know? I used to go out to the stables, like, this stable near my house, to wash my horse, Zeus. 'Cause when you ride, you know, you're supposed to take care of your animal too. That's a part of the whole responsibility aspect. So when you go out to the stable, I mean, you see certain things when you're in the stables."

I made a noise then, a thoughtful little *sure, I understand* noise.

"I think it has something to do with my dad," Mandy said. "He was really well hung. That's what my mom used to always say. Hung like a horse. You know that expression?"

I started to wonder if this wasn't maybe a practical joke. Or worse, if some undercover video–type show might have recruited Mandy. This was an era in which hidden video had become the hot new medium. Citizens found the authenticity irresistible. Real people. Real shame.

"I think that's where I made the connection," Mandy said. "Like, I drew on those feelings I had as a girl. And then I thought: But what if I died? Like if I died in a terrible accident. What would my mom do? Because we're, like, *super* close. Me and my mom."

I thought about Mandy's first story, "Home at Last." It was about a shy girl from Stamford, Connecticut, who arrives at college and feels lonely ("as lonely as a single pebble at the bottom of a vast blue sea") because her roommates decide, for no good reason, that she's a bitch and won't include her in any of their activities. But then she meets some really cool girls from another dorm and gets transferred to their dorm and finally decides that "home is wherever people are willing to get to know the true you." I looked at Mandy, who had just reached into her purse and would soon start applying lip gloss to her mouth, and started to sort of miss "Home at Last."

"I'm not interested in appropriate sex," Mandy said. "That's what the guy I was seeing was saying, the therapist. I always go for these older guys. I went for a couple of the teachers in high school. Well, one of them was a coach. It's pretty shocking how easy it is to get them. I guess some teachers are pretty desperate."

I did not say anything. I did not think about Mandy's tattoo or any other part of her. I did not watch her apply lip gloss. I remained very still. I remained very still and thought about the tapes of Clinton talking on the phone with one of his old flames. She asks him, "Do you like to eat pussy?" And he, the future President of the United States, answers: "You *bet* I do." The shock jocks had this snippet on a continuous tape loop. What a noble answer! A president who goes down! It was sad to watch those dopes in Congress mugging the guy, day after day. Thirty years ago, when JFK was getting head from whores in bathtubs, nobody made a peep.

"That's what I like about college," Mandy said. "The teachers are so much more, like, professional. And your class, especially. You give us a chance to express our feelings. Like how you talk about we shouldn't be writers. We should just tell the truth."

"Right," I said.

Mandy folded her arms across her chest. "Is it always so cold in here?"

"It's central air. Sorry."

"Yeah." She produced a shiver. "I've got, like, goose bumps."

"About the story," I said. "I do think you've got something. Take a look at my comments—"

"Can I ask you something, Mr. Lowe?" Mandy said. "Like a more personal question."

"Sure," I said. "But you know what? Let me just check to make sure there's no one else waiting."

Mandy looked me dead in the eye and I looked back at

her and a couple of seconds passed, a couple of very *long* seconds, like perhaps the longest seconds in the recorded history of my life, extremely complicated, morally uncharted seconds, white-toothed, lip-glistening seconds, abject, wave-goodbye-to-certain-sacred-principles type seconds.

Mandy nodded very slowly. "You should do that," she said. "You should check."

So I got up and walked over to the door and as I stepped past her, Mandy grazed my thigh with her hand, swept her hand down the outside of my thigh, and a great current of hope passed through my body, followed by a frisson of dread, followed by more hope, such that I began to tremble a little, more than a little, and Mandy, sensing this physiological event, let her hand settle on my knee.

She began gently to massage the anterior regions, as if checking for ligament damage, while I looked down into her face and tried to decide what sort of witness she would make in a court of law.

"I can tell you like me," Mandy said. She smiled and blew a strand of hair off her cheek. "And you want to kiss me, but you're afraid I'll say something to one of my stupid roommates and ruin the whole thing. True?"

I dipped my chin in a manner that was both a nod and a plausibly deniable non-nod.

"But why would I do that to my favorite teacher in the whole world?"

Mandy closed her eyes and made her lips into a buttery little bow. She gave my trousers a prompting tug.

Well.

I suppose I bent to kiss her, just a glancing kiss, a swift brush of my mouth across hers, but Mandy needed more than that. She grasped my thigh and let out a stagy moan and shook loose the chopstick, so that her hair fell free. There was something in these gestures, a certain rehearsed quality, that made me sad. I felt suddenly, irretrievably sorry for both of us, for Mandy, who viewed her sexuality as a bright new user option only obscurely related to her heart, and for me, who was losing hair in clumps and couldn't even give my wife a decent poking anymore. I wanted to have a good cry right then, preferably with my head nuzzled somewhere warm.

But before I could do any such thing there was a knock on the door. I leapt backwards, smashed my tailbone against the edge of my desk. The door swung open a crack and I could see Brendan Mahoney standing there with his visor in one hand and a cookie in the other. He reeked of pot.

I lunged toward him and flung the door the rest of the way, so that he could see the entire office, Mandy seated across from my desk with all her clothes on and so forth.

"Hey," he said.

"Brendan!"

"I didn't realize you were with someone."

"Just finishing!" I said.

"Hey Mandy," he said, and waved his cookie.

Mandy was already rebinding her hair, gathering up her purse. She slipped past Brendan without looking at him.

Brendan remained in the hallway.

"Did you want to come in?" I said.

"Yeah. Okay. Sure."

He stepped in the office and sat down.

"What's up?" I said.

But Brendan had spotted the antidrug poster, which showed a kid lying on the ground facedown, with his head bleeding. The legend underneath read: DRUGS SURE ARE GLAMOROUS.

"That's not mine," I said.

"It isn't?"

"No. I don't believe drugs are that bad."

Brendan seemed to consider this. "Huh," he said finally. "Yeah. I guess I'm still sort of undecided on the issue."

"Tell me why you're here," I said.

There was a long lag time on the answer. I wondered if Brendan might be under the influence of a more powerful sedative, such as rophynol, and where he might have gotten them and whether he had any in his pocket. He was now examining the naked Plato sketch.

"Is that you?" he said finally.

"Plato," I said.

"Right. Plato." He sat up and began to nod. Then he slumped down again, in that way characteristic of young men who haven't quite grown into their height.

"So," I said.

"Yeah. I guess I wanted to apologize. Like, for all the stuff in class today. Sometimes I kind of get going on an idea and just don't stop. Mandy must have been pretty pissed."

"On the contrary," I said. "She appreciated how seriously you took her work."

"I know Emily was pissed."

There was another lengthy pause. It occurred to me that I was getting something of a contact high. Everything had started moving more slowly, more interestingly. The events of the day were coming to seem somehow related. Brendan looked up at me with his sorry, bloodshot eyes.

"Me and her were involved, you know."

"Yeah?"

"Yeah. We just broke up. A couple of weeks ago."

"That's rough," I said.

"It was weird, man. I mean, I don't know if I want to lay it all out."

"Your call," I said.

"I assume, like, whatever I said would stay between us. Like, on the DL. The Down Low. Anyway, she's a nice girl.

I've got nothing against her. But she wanted to do weird stuff." Brendan sat there, fingering the top of his cookie. "She liked to touch my ass, man. Put stuff up there. Weird. She had these balls made out of, like, mercury or something. And a string of pearls. And all this lube. Man, she was the queen of lubes. She was like, 'Come on. Be an adventurer.' I told her, 'Hey, unless you're my personal physician, you don't get to fifth base.' I dunno, man. I'm from New Hampshire. You know what I mean?"

I nodded.

"She was all, like: 'Are you afraid you're gay?' And I was like, 'No. I don't like stuff put up my ass. Does that make me gay?'"

It wasn't clear whether Brendan wanted me to answer this question.

"So anyway, that's part of the reason I might have gotten sort of crazy today. Because here she is coming off all, like, puritaniacal, like, I'm so gross and I'm so sick, when the truth is she's the freak. Freaky deaky." Brendan had halfway crushed his cookie and he stared at the pieces in his hand, then crammed them into his mouth. "I just wanted to say sorry. I guess there's no need to go into detail. You probably don't need to hear this stuff, seeing as you're married and everything."

"How do you know I'm married?"

"The ring, bro."

"Right."

"How's that working for you, the marriage?"

"Fine," I said. "Why do you ask?"

"I dunno. I just figure it'd be weird to be around all these hot young chicks all the time and have the ball and chain at home."

"You learn to live with it."

We were both silent for a while. Brendan had slumped down so low his head was resting on the back of the chair. He closed his eyes and said, "I'm pretty sure Mandy Shaw wants to fuck you, dude. Man, I'd like to fuck her."

I made my thoughtful professorial noise.

"What do you want to do long term, Brendan?"

"Long term?" he said. "Probably brain surgeon."

"Don't you have to have pretty good grades for that?"

Brendan looked down at his hand and realized, with visible disappointment, that he'd already eaten his cookie. "Yeah, that's kind of the catch-22 of the situation."

"Can I ask if you're stoned, Brendan?"

"Not really anymore."

"Well, for what it's worth, I thought your comments today were very insightful."

"You did?"

"Yup."

"You weren't pissed?"

"Not at all," I said. "A for the day."

Brendan gazed at me shyly, as I imagined a child might gaze at his father upon receiving a gift. "I still kind of miss her," he said.

My own wife had loved me once so fiercely that she clung to me through the night. In the moments after love, our skin had glowed and our lungs had screamed with joy. It was her belief, though, that something had died within me, a certain capacity for tenderness. She had me convinced.

Brendan had gone a little misty on me now. "It sucks to be alone," he said. "It sucks shit."

I got up from behind my desk and looked down into his face, a smooth, open face, with so much woe still to come.

"What am I supposed to do?" he asked me. "At night, I mean."

I laid my hand on his shoulder. "Forgive her. Forgive yourself. There's no other way."

I know this sounds depressing, but it was a lovely little moment, the both of us sitting there in my office with tears pooled in our eyes.

A number of unpleasant things happened later. Nicole Buswell filed a complaint with the dean of students, alleging that my class was "overly sexualized." Rob Tway testified on my behalf. So did Mandy Shaw. But the whole thing put a cloud over me and I agreed to go on leave. My wife filed for divorce and took up with a Tae Bo instructor named Jericho. The hard-on difficulty was diagnosed as a partial stricture of the vas deferens, which required a costly and painful surgery. Clinton staggered from office, a disgraced eunuch.

But all that was still to come on the day I'm describing. On that day, Brendan Mahoney and I rose from our chairs and strolled into the dusk. It was one of those warm spring jobs that coats everything in gold and we floated through the courtyard, with its sleeping crocuses and luminous blades of grass. The cafeteria was pumping out the sweet greasy smell of calico skillet and the tall stone cathedral was dozing before us and all the students gathered in the shadows to hug struck me, just then, as beautiful creatures, freaks, all of them, with their frail bodies and fearless hearts. We could hear them kissing, wetly, to the point of collapse.

Brendan Mahoney ducked into an alcove behind the rectory. He pulled a joint from his hip pocket, lit up, and took a drag.

"You want a rip?" he said.

"Better not," I said, taking the joint.

The lovers were all around us, making their strange, gentle noises of mercy. I took my rip and Brendan nodded. "Nice," he said. "Nice form." He put his arm around me, as if we'd done something heroic together, as if the happiness within us were a puff of smoke we might hold on to forever, and he snorted like a horse, a young fearless stallion who's just shaken his bridle, and pawed the ground, and I snorted and pawed the ground too and both of us began to giggle, wildly, senselessly, and went galloping (us stallions!) off into the dusk.

I AM AS I AM

THE DEVELOPER'S HOPE had been to establish the park in Dorset Centre as a "public square" of the sort British townships once organized themselves around. The design featured a lazy slope of grass circled by a gravel pathway. In the proposed model, displayed at Village Hall, little plastic mommies pushed perambulators along this path, while a knot of boys tussled after a ball on a swathe of green. Beyond this, a man on a raised box held one arm aloft, his tiny mouth open. A group of fellow citizens stood before him in postures of thoughtful attention.

This was not, in fact, how the park looked. The village crime consultant voiced alarm at the prospect of creating an unstructured "youth magnet" environment. The open space, therefore, was somewhat reduced and converted into a par course. When, after several months, it became clear no one used the par course, a baseball field took its place. As the village fulfilled its prophecy of attenuated growth, the roads around the park widened and a new round of fretting ensued over the possibility that a child would chase a ball into traffic. The park's central location, originally embraced as a quaint communal flourish, seemed, upon sober reflection, inattentive, even reckless. The baseball field was soon encircled by a high chain-link fence.

This was why the boys of Dorset began referring to the field as the Prison Lot. They grumbled over the sense of confinement, which ran contrary to the sport's pastoral spirit. And, being children, they took up the obvious challenge: to hit a ball over the fence. In this way, they managed a collaboration that publicly confounded adult concerns. On summer afternoons, with the shadows drawn long across the grass, threads of boys in baseball mitts converged on the Prison Lot to conduct the business of childhood.

ERIC HIELMAN WAS a handsome boy and he had lived with the advantages of his looks. He was picked up and played with frequently as a baby. He made friends easily. Teachers doted on him. He had a fine jaw, his father's jaw, and eyes the green of antique glass. He was also the only boy ever to clear the Prison Lot's fence in a game situation.

Bat speed was the central issue in Eric's life. His father, who had played ball in college, explained that a major leaguer must be able to bring his bat from a motionless state to a dynamic point of contact, at waist level, in less than half a second. This required coordination of the entire body: the eye had to pick up the ball and anticipate its path, wrists and forearms had to bring the bat to the back of its swing, upper arms and shoulders had to flex and pivot, the trunk and waist had to rotate, the thighs had to transfer the weight of the lower body from the back foot to the front in a controlled lunge. It was a kind of ballet—Eric's father had said this, a bit dreamily, quickly adding that the goal was to "maximize bat speed," that without the cooperation of any one part the swing would fail.

The most frustrating aspect of a baseball swing, Eric's father said, was that it had to be *intuitive*. Eric, who was clever enough but only nine years old, shook his head. "You can't think about the swing," his father said. "You can't tell your body to do all these things I'm talking about. You have to let your body figure it out on its own."

Eric spent hours in the backyard practicing, hoping to familiarize his body with the mechanics of the swing, to bleed the process of thought, and listening for the sound of his father's car in the front driveway. Inevitably, his mother ordered him inside before his father arrived, citing darkness.

Like his father, Eric was tall and solidly built. By his tenth year, he had developed an exceptional swing: smooth and explosive. When he stepped to the plate, the infielders edged back. The outfielders positioned themselves on the warning track and turned to one another and spat. If the ball sailed over the fence, they would have to retrieve it.

Eric himself took little notice of these adjustments. He thought of nothing in the batter's box, tried to think of nothing. This was the key to success in life, as his father had intimated. "The whole problem with this place," his father would say, eyeing the groomed lawns of Dorset Centre, "is too damn much thinking." Eric thought about the space at the far end of the park, where the girls now played dolls on the gazebo. And sometimes he imagined his father there, standing on a box and telling the people of Dorset what he really thought of the place. He envisioned this as a heroic moment, one they would secretly share, though he knew his mother would never allow such a thing to transpire.

AMONG THE PLAYERS were younger and weaker boys. Bill Bellamy was a sad third category: ungainly. He lacked coordination, and worse, lacked the good grace to remove himself from games. A doughy, red-haired boy, Bellamy was so pale his veins appeared to run green. He failed as a player, but always with an exuberance that refused to recognize his failure. He held the bat like a girl, fists apart, and came around late, even on slow pitches. He was a loss in the field, logy in his reflexes, incapable of tracking. Second base or right field were his, unless there were enough fielders, in which case he was happily excluded from the game.

The notion of placing him behind the plate was a new one. Perhaps he would do less damage as a catcher.

The experiment was a failure. Bill Bellamy was frightened of the ball and twisted away, holding his mitt out as if to shield his eyes from a small explosion, then chuckling to himself as he lumbered to the backstop. By the time Eric Hielman came up to bat, on the long last day of summer, players were yelling for a new catcher. More kids had arrived. Bill Bellamy was expendable.

Down at first base Stevie Hayes was calling out "new catcher new catcher" and Matt Anderson, the shortstop, took up the chant. They were the best players in the game, besides Eric, and the others joined in. Eric stood at the plate and waited, trying to avoid thought. But hesitation was the ally of thought; it muddied instinct. The pitcher, Jamie Blake, looked at Eric.

"Just pitch the ball," Eric hollered.

It hadn't been his intention to make a noble gesture, only to move the game along so he could take his turn at bat. He felt strong today, and the spot where he stood, at the center of this enclosed diamond, emphasized his strength. As he squared his shoulders and watched Jamie Blake dip into his windup, he experienced the euphoria of perfected focus. The other boys scattered across the brown and green, the hovering sky, the smell of bubble gum and linseed oil on leather, the new tar of distant roads: all these seemed a part of his brightly appointed future. Behind him, Bill Bellamy said, "Thanks Eric," said this with a goofy conviviality he seemed to feel was shared, and stooped forward on his clumsy cleats, hoping, apparently, to offer his gratitude with a pat on the back or a handshake or some other gesture of touch, which Eric Hielman never noticed.

The pitch came in, one of Blake's halfhearted sliders, and Eric could see that it would not break; the rotation was insufficient. It would sit up and wait to be drilled. Eric's body would execute this and was already beginning to execute this, wrists and arms and trunk and legs acting in concert to pull the swing around, into abrupt dynamic motion, a single whipcord arc beginning over his left shoulder and ending as he stepped forward and felt his bat explode into Bill Bellamy's head.

HE DID NOT understand that this was what had happened. Not immediately. What he understood was only a truncation of the bat's natural progress. He had come up against something, a spongy feeling he would recognize later as flesh giving way to wood. The pitch came in at waist level, but he was off-balance now, as a result of this obstacle, this thing, and falling toward the plate, the trance of his swing broken and shouts knifing in from the field and, on the face of Jamie Blake, a pinched look he had never seen before. From behind home plate came the heavy sound of a body falling without resistance.

Eric stumbled then righted himself. He turned around. Bill Bellamy lay on the ground, half-curled. His shirt rode up over his belly. An arm lay over his forehead. But even obscured, it was clear his skull was wrongly shaped. His orange hair had begun to mat with dark fluid. His feet twitched. "Bellamy," Eric said. There was no response.

Jamie Blake and Stevie Hayes and the others were now gathered around home plate and Eric turned to them and saw that they sagged back an inch or two. Jamie looked down and Eric realized that he still held the bat in his hand and that the bat was cracked. Not a deep crack, one that he would be able to tape if he wanted to use the bat for practice, which of course was no way to be thinking at the moment. He dropped the bat.

One of the younger kids, Tom Sevrance, began whimpering. "Blood," he said. "Blood." He pointed to the small puddle beneath Bill Bellamy's head, as if it were important to convince some adult just out of view. Without a word, Stevie Hayes set off for the gate and Matt Anderson flew after him, mitts thumping against their hips. The others followed. Only Jamie Blake remained with Eric, trapped in the grim duty of attending to Bill Bellamy.

"He's hurt," Jamie said. "He's really fucking hurt."

Eric said: "Bellamy? Bellamy, can you hear me?"

"Blood," Jamie said. "He's fucking bleeding from his head."

"Okay. Calm down. An ambulance is going to come. They'll call an ambulance."

"We should do something, man," Jamie said. He had begun to cry and now fell to his knees and pounded his head into the dirt. "Fuck, man. Fuck. His head, man. Fuck."

Eric considered this idea, of doing something. He looked at Bill Bellamy and noticed that his eyes were closed, but his stomach was moving, quivering with fast, shallow breaths. He knew about CPR from a film in school (a firm thrust of the palms below the sternum, use your weight) and, from swimming certification, he knew about mouth-to-mouth resuscitation (clear the breathing passages and form a seal over the mouth, four breaths then a break). But he knew nothing about head injuries. They hadn't gone over that: what to do when you have smashed someone's head in with a baseball bat.

Jamie was on his hands and knees, making retching noises.

"Calm down," Eric said. "He's breathing. He'll be alright. We just have to wait until the ambulance comes."

"Fuck," Jamie said and retched again and continued crying. "It was like he was down before you hit him."

Eric could see Stevie Hayes and the others crossing the

street that led to their homes, darting up front walks. He turned to Bill Bellamy and crouched. "Bellamy," he said. "The ambulance is coming." A sharp ammoniac scent rose from the body. Its feet continued to twitch.

Jamie was muttering to himself. "Fuck, the way you hit him. Like his head was, like, fuck, like *crack*."

Eric didn't like the way Jamie was saying this, as if he, Eric, had known Bellamy was there, or had had some control over the situation. "You shouldn't have thrown a pitch if he wasn't set."

"Me?" Jamie reared up on his knees. His face was webbed with snot. "You were the one, Eric. Shit. You were the one who swung."

This was the difference, Eric realized: Jamie had seen it happen. This was why he was so upset. He had been a witness. "Okay," Eric said. "He'll be alright. We just need to wait until the ambulance comes. We have to stay here and explain." The two of them said nothing. They looked at Bill Bellamy every few seconds; they did not look at one another.

"Maybe we should turn him over," Jamie said.

"No," Eric said. "I don't think we should touch him. It's serious, a serious thing."

"I know it's serious," Jamie said. "Shit. I know."

Now the sound of a siren rose and dipped. It was not a familiar sound in Dorset Centre and it made the dogs, labs and shepherds mostly, howl. The ambulance companies had trouble in Dorset, with its cul-de-sacs and speed bumps and winding streets. Eric could hear the siren swell, then recede.

A group of girls left their place at the far end of the park and headed toward the field, squinting into the low sun and pointing. Jamie's younger sister spotted him. "What happened?" she screamed. "Jamie, are you okay? Is Jamie okay?"

"I'm okay," Jamie said, but, at the sight of his sister, he began crying again.

"He's fine, Kelly," Eric said.

"What happened? Who's hurt?" The girls collected at the fence along the third-base line.

"Bill Bellamy," Eric said. "But he's going to be alright." Eric heard one of the girls say, "Bill Smellamy," and the others laughed. "Just go home now," he said.

The girls were suspicious of being shooed away, but they sagged back once the ambulance appeared, howling with lights. The truck jumped the curve and drove right up to the fence. A trio of men burst out of the back with a gurney and hustled across the field. Eric had expected they would want to know what happened, but they ran right past him and Jamie and hunched over Bill Bellamy and one of them said, "Good God," and another ran back to the truck for more supplies. A short man with a beard, obviously the one in charge, said, "Is there any way to get our truck onto this field?"

"I don't think so," Eric said. "There's just the gate."

"Great. Great planning." He wore latex gloves, the fingers of which were already stained crimson. They eased Bill Bellamy onto his side and wedged a board under his floppy body and raised him up. One of the paramedics started an IV and a second held a compress to his head. The reddish dirt from which he had been lifted was darkened by blood; it looked like chocolate cake batter. The medics carried the gurney gingerly. "Go home," the man with the beard called out. He slid the body inside, the gurney collapsing.

Eric felt a sense of betrayal at having lost sight of Bill Bellamy. He had somehow assumed he was going with the medics, that they would need him for something. He and Jamie walked home in silence.

Eric turned into his driveway. "See ya."

"Right." Jamie had his head down.

"You okay?"

"Yeah." Jamie walked on and Eric knew then they would never again speak about what had happened, not to each other.

Eric himself was distressed to discover his most urgent memory of the incident: he had caught sight of Bill Bellamy's face as they attended to him. It seemed to him the boy had been smiling faintly.

· · ·

He closed the door lightly, but his mother heard him come in, as she always did, and hung up the phone and rushed toward him. She was smoking, a vice she disdained in public, but practiced with a peculiar vengeance at home. Her words cut through the smoke. "Are you okay, honey? Marcia Hayes called and told me about the accident. That's what the ambulance was about, wasn't it? Did you do this? Hit the Bellamy boy with a bat? Marcia says it was an accident, that everybody knows it was an accident. What happened?"

"He was the catcher," Eric said. "I was at the plate. Jamie pitched the ball. I didn't see him—"

"Jamie? Jamie Blake?"

"Yeah. I was just watching the pitch and when I swung, the bat hit him. Bellamy."

Eric's mother took a sharp drag on her cigarette and Eric found himself worrying, absurdly, that her ash would fall on the rug. "Why did Jamie pitch the ball if Bellamy was in the way?"

"I don't know."

"Why was Bill in the way if you were swinging? Isn't the catcher supposed to be back, out of the way?"

"Yeah."

"How badly is he hurt?"

"I don't know. Pretty bad. His head was bleeding. A lot."

"What did the paramedics say?"

"Nothing. They just took him away."

Her brow crimped and her lips began forming silent words. This was what she did during awkward social situations. "Nothing," she said quietly. Then, to him, she said, "Are you okay?"

"I guess." He wondered if he would start to cry.

"This was just an accident," she said quickly. "You did nothing wrong." She moved forward and hugged him, her arms caging him briefly, the smoke from her cigarette ribboning between her fingers. "Please stay inside, Eric. If the phone rings, let the machine pick up. I need to get your brother from soccer. You mustn't worry. Do you understand?"

The phone did ring several times, the distressed tones of one or another mother on the machine. Eric wanted to speak to someone, his father or Stevie Hayes, or even his little brother. He thought about heading outside, but was suddenly frightened someone would see him, that there would be a commotion. The feeling reminded him of having the chicken pox, a kind of quarantine. He called his father's office but there was no answer. He checked the fridge; the maid had left a lasagna. He turned the TV on and watched music videos with the volume on high.

His mother took forever getting home. He knew that

she had been making the rounds, gathering information. She was berating Mikey over something as she entered, but smiled when she saw him. "We'll have pizza tonight, okay?"

"Hey Eric," Mikey said. "What happened? I heard you hit Bill Bellamy in the head with a bat. Crack! Mom said. And Mrs. Middleton. What happened?"

Eric's mother turned on her younger son and swatted him, hard, on the behind. "What did I just tell you? Leave your brother *alone*. Do you understand me? Get those muddy shoes off this instant and take a shower." Mikey's face flushed. He made for the stairs. Only recently had he advanced past the stage of unashamed crying.

"Maybe we should call the Bellamys," Eric said. "To find out how Bill is doing. I could call. To apologize."

His mother didn't appear to hear this.

"Or we could call Dad," Eric said.

His mother looked up from the phone book. "Your father is busy. I'll talk to him when he gets home."

ERIC SLIPPED INTO Mikey's room. His brother was still in his soccer uniform, grass stains on his shorts. He could hear his mother downstairs, murmuring into the phone.

"Mom said for me not to bother you."

"Don't worry about it," Eric said.

Mikey glanced up nervously. "What happened?" he said softly.

Eric told his brother the story, not embellishing, only re-stating the events from the time he stepped to the plate un-til the paramedics left. The tip of Mikey's tongue hung over his bottom lip as he listened. "Mom told Mrs. Middleton that Jamie Blake shouldn't have thrown the ball," he said fi-nally. "She said he's hyperactive."

"It wasn't Jamie's fault," Eric said.

"Bill Bellamy should have been back more. He's the catcher. Only a fat retard doesn't know that."

Eric knew his brother had heard these names from older kids, maybe from Eric himself. He looked at Mikey for a long time. His brother had their mother's eyes, dark and pretty and jumpy when faced down. He hoped that Mikey would understand the shame of his words, that he might offer the apology of silence. But Mikey giggled sheepishly. "There's nothing funny," Eric said. "Don't say stuff like that about Bill Bellamy, okay? Bellamy's hurt. How would you like it if you got hurt and someone teased you?"

"I didn't get hurt," Mikey said.

ERIC HAD SLEPT over at Bill Bellamy's once, a year ago. A birthday slumber party. Bellamy's parents had made elab-orate preparations, sending out fancy invitations, phoning a list of mothers. They had wanted to make sure enough kids would show up.

Mrs. Bellamy, a birdlike woman who hummed to herself, handed each child a bag of goodies at the door. Mr. Bellamy fetched sodas. The boys sat around in Bill's room, playing an old computer video game. Bill's little sister, Tracy, kept sticking her head in the door and running away laughing. Like her mother, she was slightly walleyed. Mr. Bellamy announced that chow was on and served up pizza he had made himself. Rather than pepperoni, the pie had little sliced up hot dogs on it.

The Bellamys lived on the outskirts of Dorset Centre, in a portion of the development known as the Annex. It had been built after the initial developer sold his interests to independent contractors. The lots were smaller, the homes crammed together, and none of them had pools. The Bellamy house seemed to slant.

The boys managed to escape the house for a midnight game of tackle the pill, and a few whispered of heading home. Bill remained oblivious, lost in the happy enthusiasms of the birthday boy. Cake was served upon their return. The boys who had spoken of leaving settled instead for the distractions of torturing Bill in his sleep. They soaked his fingers in warm water and put toothpaste in his ear. If he minded these pranks, he said nothing. When the boys woke the next morning, Mr. Bellamy was in the kitchen, his loamy body wrapped in an apron, a spatula in one hand. "Who wants griddle cakes?" he called out.

"I do," Bill said. He pulled the dog, a mangy terrier, onto his lap. Eric was horrified to see fleas squirming on the dog's belly.

Tracy burst out laughing. "Billy has fleas," she squealed. "Billy has fleas."

ERIC'S FATHER DIDN'T get home until after nine. He looked rumpled, as he usually did, like a slightly deflated version of the crisp, well-dressed man who left in the morning. Eric had been hanging around the foyer. But his mother headed him off. "Don't jump on your father. Let me talk to him."

Eric began to protest, but her face was smooth with the promise of an outburst. "Go to your room, Eric. He'll come up."

In a few minutes, he heard his father's car start and he moved to the window and watched it depart. His mother came into his room. She had a cigarette in one hand and a drink in the other.

"Where's dad going?"

"Honey, sit down for a minute. Your father is going to the Bellamys. He wants to find out what's going on."

"Why can't I go with him?"

"No, honey. This is something serious. I know it was an

accident, honey. We know that. But we don't know how people are going to react. Your father is a smart man. He works all day helping people solve arguments. So let's let him speak with the Bellamys."

"But I was the one who was there. It was my fault."

Eric's mother tensed her jaw. "It was not your fault, honey. Don't say that. Do not say that."

"But I was there. And I know Mr. Bellamy."

"After your father returns and we know the situation, you can write a card to them. A get-well card." Eric wanted to tell her that he was scared, that he *needed* to say he was sorry, but he was afraid she would try to embrace him again.

His father returned a half hour later. Downstairs, his mother launched her interrogation. His father said: "Enough, Jeanie. Let me see him." There was a knock on the door. His father's long body angled into the room. "Hey."

"Hey."

"Rough day, huh?"

"Yeah."

His father sat on the bed. "Bill Bellamy is in the hospital. He'll be there for a while. The doctors say he's had a hemorrhage of some kind. That's like a problem inside his head. They need to wait for the swelling to go down." His father rubbed his eyes. Eric thought about the moment of impact, that spongy feeling. "They won't know anything until the swelling goes down. There's a chance, if he hemorrhages again . . . but he probably won't. The doctors will know more when the swelling goes down."

"How are the Bellamys?"

"Well, I mean, they're upset. Upset. But they know it wasn't your fault, kiddo. They know it was an accident. Are *you* okay?"

Eric nodded.

"Your mother says you've been very brave."

"It feels weird, Dad."

"I know it does. I know."

Eric looked at his father's profile, lined by the light in the hallway. The patches of flesh under his eyes were swollen and colored with sleeplessness. It didn't seem fair that his father should have to suffer this, that either of them—it wasn't fair. He felt sorry for his father, and he felt that it would be unfair to add his own tears to his father's burdens. Still, he wanted his father to stay. Not to comfort him, just to sit beside him until he could fall asleep. He heard his mother's footsteps and then her voice at the door and then his father's body rising up and being led away.

Eric stood in the doorway of his room, listening to the conversation floating up the stairs. He was supposed to be asleep.

"The man's only son," his father said.

"Yes, I know. You've already said that. Now listen to what I'm saying: we don't *know* these people."

"He's a teacher. He teaches math to eighth graders."

"What do you think teachers get paid, Stan? Honestly." Eric heard her drop ice cubes in a glass. "You're too damn trusting. These people, I mean, look where they live. And you know as well as anyone how victims are. They want to make *somebody* pay."

"Do we have to talk about this now, Jeanie?" His father sounded tired.

"And that Blake boy—"

"It's not really appropriate—"

"They give him that drug, Stan, for hyperactive children. He has an attention disorder. Barbara brought it up at PTA, made a big fuss. She wanted the district to hold some kind of sensitivity workshop or something. What's that drug called?"

"Ritalin."

"Yes, Ritalin. He takes Ritalin. And the Bellamy boy himself had asthma. Dr. Springer told him not to play organized sports, warned him not to. Cheryl told me herself. That's why they keep him out of soccer. But of course they can't stop him from playing in that damn park." Eric heard in his mother's voice a familiar enthusiasm for tragedy. She spoke the same way to the morning newspaper. "He should have been wearing some protection," she said. "The catcher is supposed to have a mask and a helmet."

"Not in a pickup game."

"In any kind of game."

"That's not how it works," his father said.

"That's how it should work, Stan. Look what's happened."

"These things happen, honey."

"Not to people who are careful."

"Yes they do, Jeanie. They just happen."

"Okay," she said. "Let's just stop this. We're going in circles. Don't get up. Sit." He heard his mother pad across to where they kept the liquor. "All I'm saying is that we should be prepared for anything that might happen. I've made a few calls, just to see what the other kids are saying. You know how kids are, Stan. They make up stories. Blood makes them crazy."

There was a pause.

"I never liked that field," his father said.

"Yes, all that traffic. It's a death trap."

His father sighed and clinked his ice cubes. "That's not it, Jeanie. That's not what I mean. You can't plan everything out. That's what I mean. They should have just left it a big patch of grass."

"Or the par course," his mother said. "I liked the par course."

PUBLIC DISCUSSION OF the matter closed at home. But it remained very much alive at school. Eric's friends all wanted to reenact the event, its mysterious violent glamour. After a few days, Eric began eating his lunch inside. He could hear the other boys who had been there at the Prison Lot, Jamie Blake and Stevie Hayes and the rest, discussing the particulars, the angle of impact, the body's prone position.

Miss Weeks, the fifth-grade teacher, announced that Bill Bellamy was "doing fine" and had the class send a card signed by all of them. Eric sent a card of his own, carrying the envelope to the village post office and mailing it himself. The item in the *Dorset Register* mentioned only that William Bellamy, age ten, had been injured in a baseball accident. He was in critical condition.

At home, Eric could hear his mother worrying the incident on the phone, her voice low and raspy. She was smoking more than ever, hiding the smell from company with air freshener that hung about in clouds. His father treated him kindly, laying a hand on his shoulder, telling him to keep his chin up. But he appeared helpless before the larger duties of concern, worn out by his days at the office. He rarely arrived home in time for dinner.

On Sunday morning, his mother walked into the TV room and announced that the family would be attending church.

Mikey made a face. "Church?"

"I want both of you in your suits. No arguments."

She wore a new dress, dark blue, and makeup and high-heel shoes. His father wore a suit as well. They drove in silence. Eric wondered if the Bellamys would be there. His suit felt too tight.

In the parking lot, Eric's mother went to find friends.

"Dad," Mikey said. "Why are we here?"

"We're here for church, Mike."

"But why? It's not Christmas."

Eric's father dropped into a crouch and addressed his son face-to-face. "Now come on, Mike. Don't start up. We've come to church to worship. You should know better than to misbehave. Try to act like your brother. You don't see him complaining, do you?"

His mother met them at the entrance and marched them up the center aisle to the front pew. Eric felt sure the Bellamys would join them there. He began rehearsing in his head what he would say to them. How sorry he was, how worried and sorry.

But then the hymns began. The minister, a stout man in a purple robe, delivered a rambling sermon about Jesus and the Pharisees. "Jesus wore a simple frock and from this drew his hand, and said, 'Let no blood stain the hands of an innocent.' And, you see, he forgave them their scorn, because, because you see, it was the scorn of ignorance." He said this in such a distracted tone, though, that Eric imagined he was terribly hungry. Mikey fell asleep; he yipped softly when their mother pinched him.

"Before we depart," the minister said, "I would like the congregation to say a prayer for William Bellamy, and the family of William Bellamy, of Dorset Centre, who, as some of you may know, was, is still, in the hospital. In fact, Mrs. Janine, or Jeanie Hielman, also of Dorset Centre, has volunteered to lead the congregation in prayer."

Eric's mother ascended the altar and gazed into the crowd, past the astonished faces of her sons, and said, "Lord in Heaven, please see William to a safe recovery, that his family might rest easier. Let us all pray for this. We are praying, my family, my boys—" Her voice cracked and she had to halt. "My boys and I, for William and his family." She stifled another sob and returned to her seat.

On the ride home, she said: "We should do that more often."

"No we shouldn't," Mikey said, though he said this quietly, to himself, with a child's accidental sense of purpose.

BILL BELLAMY DID not recover. Instead, the hospital announced what everyone had known for some time: he had fallen into a coma. The following weeks brought an odd silence. Nothing was said about the incident itself, but it informed much of what went on in Dorset Centre. An ordinance was passed requiring kids to wear protective gear when they played athletics in Dorset Park. But the kids, without any really discussion of the matter, abandoned the Prison Lot. The small, fenced field that had once been the center of a communal life to Eric and his friends gathered leaves.

Mrs. Bellamy (never, according to Eric's mother, a stable person) took to riding Bill's bicycle through the development, trailing after her daughter. Both wore pigtails. From time to time, Eric saw Mr. Bellamy returning from the junior high in his old station wagon, staring vacantly ahead at the road. If he recognized Eric, he gave no indication.

Bill Bellamy died in late October, a few days before Halloween. Eric's mother, who learned of this almost immediately, said nothing until his father came home. She sent Mikey to bed and sat both of them down. "The doctors said there was really nothing left to do. I called the Bellamys to express our condolences. I asked about sending a floral arrangement. Bill's father said they have set up a memorial fund. I told him we would contribute, of course." She put out her cigarette and straightened her armrest cover and looked at Eric. "I know this has been a difficult time for you, Eric. You feel responsible. That is only natural. But you must realize that this is not your fault. No one blames you, so you mustn't blame yourself." She got up from the couch and went to Eric and grappled him into a hug. "We love you for who you are," she said.

Eric's father seemed caught off guard. "Your mother is right," he said, glancing at the crystal decanter atop the liquor cabinet. "It's very sad. For this to have happened. Sad. But you can't, you can't let this, you know, stop you . . ." His mouth continued moving, but no sound came out. He appeared to have lost his place.

"Yes," his mother said. "We feel, we both feel, that you've put yourself through quite a lot over this. Too much. We understand if you are sad. And especially now, with this. It is terribly sad. Tragic. But you mustn't do this to yourself. Remember how much you used to like baseball? And you don't play at all anymore, now. Mrs. Blake and Mrs. Hayes, they say, you know, they don't see you much anymore. And the boys miss you too. You are such a successful boy, so smart and handsome. So popular." Abruptly, she got up and went to the kitchen and returned holding a cake pan.

Eric glanced at his father, who shook his head.

"Remember how we used to make a cake for Halloween, before you were old enough to go trick-or-treating? And you could request the colors? You always wanted green cake with orange frosting, remember? Such silly colors. When I heard this, about poor Bill Bellamy, I was quite upset, as you can imagine. And I needed something to distract myself, I guess, and I found myself making a chocolate cake. It's been years since I've baked, Lord knows, but I just found myself making it. These aren't the colors you requested, but I did the best I could."

The cake, lettered in orange and green, read: I AM AS I AM. "I put those words on as a reminder, Eric. A reminder that we love you for who you are. If you're hungry, you can have a piece before bed. I know it's against house rules, but I won't tell if you won't." She smiled tightly and hurried to the kitchen, where Eric heard her clattering for a knife. She returned with a small square of cake on a plate, which she set before him. The cake was yellow. Alma, the maid, must have made it.

"I'm not really hungry," he said.

"If you have a piece it will be like you are giving yourself a reward. A reward for being so brave about all this." Eric's mother looked at his father. "It's the message that's most important, Eric," she said brightly. "The message. Isn't that right?"

Eric waited for his father to say something, to break the silence that settled over them. But he only looked again at the bourbon, this time with a pitiable longing.

And so Eric picked up his fork and chewed the cake and swallowed and thanked his mother and told her he understood and not to worry and climbed the stairs and lay in bed and waited for sleep. He waited a long time. He heard his mother and father below, her shrill incantations, his drowsy murmurs, the clink of his ice cubes, the snap of her lighter. He heard them climb the stairs and go about their before-bed rituals. He wondered if his father would come to say good night.

After a time, Eric stopped wondering. It was dark and quiet and when the salty taste of nausea came, he felt relieved. He ran to the bathroom and stooped and his stomach heaved. Someone hurried into the hallway. Eric shut the door and locked it.

He turned the light out and touched his forehead to the cool rim of the toilet and let his mother's voice bounce off the door. A whitish silence rose around him. Then a green stretch of lawn slowly unfurled and at the far end, clear as could be, stood Bill Bellamy. His face was hideously swollen, disfigured in a manner Eric recognized at once as permanent. Bellamy was nonetheless determined to speak. He offered a slight bow and clambered onto the raised platform and addressed Eric in a voice that swirled the leaves of the Prison Lot and traveled to every well-tended corner of Dorset Centre. "I am as I am," Bill Bellamy said. "Remember that. Remember me."

A HAPPY DREAM

HENRY WAS OUT in front of the Brattle waiting for his sister, Marla, who was late, on the verge of standing him up actually, when he saw a woman zip across the street on a ten-speed bike. This was crazy. It was early February, the roads were still layered with dirty snow. The woman bonked into a parking meter, locked the bike, pulled her hat off, and there was her hair, a cascade of the stuff. She looked around briskly and made straight for Henry.

"You must be Michael," she said. "I'm Kate."

This was a pretty woman. Not beautiful. Not gorgeous. But then, Henry was all done with gorgeous. He'd just been dumped by a gorgeous woman. Or, well, a year ago he'd been dumped. And anyway, this woman, this pretty Kate, with her hair and her big, lovely nose, she was looking into his eyes expectantly and he didn't even want to see Marla, that was the truth, with her terrible social worker pity face and her cheery advice, *You need to get out there more, give yourself a chance,* blah-blah-blah.

Henry smiled shyly. "Call me Mike," he said.

AFTER THE MOVIE, they went to a bar. Kate ordered a gimlet.

"What's a gimlet?" Henry said.

"I don't know. I just like saying gimlet. Gimlet-gimlet-gimlet." She swept her hair into a bun. "So anyway, Laurie told me you're a firefighter. What's that *like*, Mike?"

Henry paused and looked around and swallowed.

"Oh," he said. "You know. Hot. Awfully hot."

Kate laughed. She had a terrific laugh, loud and a little throaty.

The drinks arrived and Henry gulped at his. "The thing is," he said, "there's really not as much action as you might think. Mostly, it's just sitting around the station. Folks are pretty good about fire safety these days."

Kate looked a little disappointed.

"That's not to say there haven't been some close calls," he said.

"What's the most dangerous fire you ever fought?"

"The most dangerous fire I've ever fought? Huh. Let me think about that one." Henry was pretty sure he was going to hell. On the other hand, he felt glorious, alive in a way he hadn't for months. "I guess, well, a couple of years ago there was this four-alarm over at Haviland Candy. They were working double shifts for Valentine's and someone must have fallen asleep. These big copper vats of chocolate exploding all over the place and flames licking at the marshmallows. Corn syrup is highly flam-mable, you know."

"My God!" Kate was running her swizzle stick along the cleft in her chin. "Were you okay?"

"A touch of smoke inhalation. No big deal. But enough about me. Tell me what *you* do."

So now Henry was following Kate home. Kate who was 27 years old and performed improv sketch comedy and worked as a chimney sweep to pay the bills. She was on her bike and she rode like an absolute maniac. Henry had trouble keeping up with her—and he was in a car.

And yet, he was utterly captivated by her recklessness, the way she darted in and out of traffic, flung herself around corners, her tires sending up strings of slush. Henry wished that Marla could see him now: a make-believe fire-fighter running red lights in pursuit of a sexy, slightly soused chimney sweep. Marla who was always saying how "risk averse" he was. ("Not risk averse," he told her. "Anti heartbreak. There's a difference.")

Then Kate went down, hard, under the wheels of a pass-ing bus. It happened so quickly Henry didn't even have time to react, though, oddly, he was sort of reacting even as he thought this, mourning her death and the life together they had missed, the long, searching conversations and, maybe even more than that, the absolutely superb sex they might someday have had and he even began to cry a little, there in his unheated Honda, as he thought about the cute little babies, two or three of them at least, all with her nose, that they would never raise.

BUT NO, THAT wasn't it. She'd merely slipped *past* the bus. She was still alive—alive!—and wheeling onto a side street. He pulled up behind her and leapt out of the car.

"I thought you'd been, that bus—"

She was under the streetlamp, flushed, panting a little, ravishing.

"I just like to let the drivers know who's boss." Kate grinned. "Besides, you're a firefighter, right? You know all that paramedics stuff. Mouth-to-mouth." A light snow drifted down and fell on her hair and he wanted to tell her, right then, no, he wasn't a firefighter, he was a sous-chef, a lonely, risk-averse sous-chef, but desire was surging through him now and the heart needed these things, these moments of grand drama. He thought: I will die if I don't kiss her.

He leaned in and kissed her, lightly. His fingertips touched her cheek. She tasted of gimlet, lime juice and the sharp bite of gin, and her eyes were still closed when she pulled away, as if she were in the midst of a happy dream.

"I usually hate blind dates," she whispered. "But this was

really, you know . . ." and then she kissed him again, harder, and her belly came against his and now Henry was fairly certain he was going to hell.

"What's the matter?" she said. "Is it, I mean, Laurie told me about your wife. Is that what it is, Mike? Are you still grieving?"

Henry sighed, elaborately and through his nose. He was really very unhappy. "Listen Kate, I'm not . . . I'm not the guy you were supposed to meet, this Mike guy. I'm just—how to explain this?—I'm just a guy who saw you and, you know, you looked so brave and pretty . . . wow. What a jerk. I'm sorry." He began to consider how he would react if she slapped his face. Would he cry? Was she a good slapper?

Kate stood there, swaying in the lamplight. "I know," she said finally.

"What?"

"I know. Marla told me—"

"Marla? What do you mean Marla told you . . ." But now Henry could see the situation. His sister had recruited this woman, or, God, maybe even hired her. Oh, this was pathetic, truly pathetic. Henry began clubbing himself on the head. "Did she pay you? Please tell me she didn't pay you."

Kate seemed to be trying not to laugh. "Please stop hitting yourself," she said, and grabbed his arm.

"You're not really a chimney sweep, are you?" Henry said quietly.

"Bike messenger, actually."

"Do you think I'm loathsome and disgusting?"

Kate looked at him again, her eyes green and quite serious now. "No, I like a man who can think on his feet. Let's try another kiss. I mean it, Mike. I've never kissed a real firefighter."

LINCOLN, ARISEN

Sleep hath its own world. —Byron

ON MARCH 14, 1865, with the war drawing to a close and the cherry trees budding, Lincoln dispatches Under Secretary Dole to convey a message along to Douglass, inviting him to take tea at the Soldier's Home.

Douglass removes the sheet of foolscap from its dainty envelope. His hair, which in official portraits will take the appearance of a bald eagle perching atop his head, dips toward his brow. "Is this a prank, Dole?"

"No sir. The president requests your company."

"My company?"

"I should think that apparent."

Douglass frowns. Nearby, a clock tolls six. He looks about in agitation. "But I have an engagement this evening, a speech."

"I see." Dole turns back to his carriage.

"I haven't time to cancel, sir. A hall has been rented; tickets issued." Rather too ardently, Douglass grasps Dole's sleeve. "Don't you see? I should be most honored to take tea with our beloved president. It is only this duty which compels me . . ."

Dole glances dubiously at Douglass's hand and nods to his driver.

"Perhaps on another occasion!" Douglass says. He is now half jogging alongside the carriage. "Perhaps—"

"Of course," murmurs Dole, as his hand draws the curtain shut.

LINCOLN IS TIRED of nobility. It has been years since he felt a single breeze of contentment. This he blames on nobility. Rectitude exhausts his every part. Days wash past in a torrent of reports and decisions. He peers at memoranda by lamplight, until the letters dance about like pickaninnies. At night, strange dreams press themselves upon him. Upon waking, he glances around his darkened bedroom and feels dread settling onto his skin like black damp.

I was happy once, he thinks: what on earth has happened?

"SO THIS IS the famous Mississippi?"

Lincoln nods, levers the flatboat toward the soft current at the river's center. They have just passed Red Wing.

His companion snorts.

"Yes?"

"I should have thought it wider."

"Give her a chance, Douglass. Rivers must be given a chance."

SENATOR POMEROY ESCORTS Douglass to the executive wing. Lincoln is in the antechamber to his office, on hands and knees, rooting among papers scattered on the floor. Pomeroy coughs discreetly. Lincoln rises, his legs seeming to unfold then unfold again, until he towers over Pomeroy, whose face shines like a small pink seashell.

"Mr. President," Pomeroy says, "may I present—"

"I know who he is, Senator." A forelock droops over Lincoln's eyes. He quietly bids the others from the room and sets a hand on Douglass's shoulder. "Seward has told me all about you. Sit down. I am glad to see you."

For the next hour, Douglass conveys the concerns of his race regarding military pay, commendations, the treatment of those captured by Confederates. Lincoln issues a pledge here, a vague promise there. Each man's posture is stiff, cautious.

There is a lengthy silence during which, it seems to Douglass, the entirety of a December dusk fills the jalousie windows behind Lincoln's desk. "I have the sense we have met somewhere before," Lincoln says. "Somewhere without all of this." He gestures at the dark wainscoting of his office, the massive leather chairs.

. . .

LINCOLN TAKES HIS shoes off and cuffs his trousers. His tufted, coppery feet give him the appearance of a forest thing, an ogre. He stares at Douglass. "Take off that ridiculous garb," he says. "It is hot enough to melt a rail tie."

Douglass unbuttons his waistcoat, untabs the collar, folds them crisply. He removes his cuff links—a gift from the New England Freedmen Association—and scans the wooden deck, shading his eyes. "Have you no chifforobe?"

DOUGLASS IN FANEUIL HALL. He stares at the puff pastry brought to him by Garrison. The cream of the abolitionist movement swirls around him: young men in golden spectacles, women in elaborate hoop dresses. Well-meaning folk agog at his capacity for speech. He pokes at the pastry, his finger sinking in. A great many people seem to want to talk to him at once.

"Douglass! Where is Douglass?"

"The proclamation's been issued!"

"Find Douglass!"

"Here he is. Speak Douglass! Speak!"

I am kept, Douglass thinks. As kept as china in an antique cabinet.

IN A WEST WING ceremony, Secretary of the Treasury Chase presents Lincoln with a newly minted twenty-dollar bill. The president holds the note up to the light. "What a signature Mr. Spinner has," he says. "But it must take him hours to sign every bill. Tell me, how does he manage it?"

Chase lets out a laugh.

"What is funny, Chase?"

"Surely you realize, Mr. President."

"Realize what?"

"Spinner's signature, sir; it is engraved on the plate."

"*Engraved?*"

"Yes."

"What, then, is to keep a thief from stealing these plates? Or one of your staff from printing extras?"

Chase stares at him, unsure what to say. "But there are safeguards," he stammers.

Lincoln shakes his head. "This thing frightens me," he murmurs. "Not even our names are kept authentic any longer."

LINCOLN RESTS HIS weight on the long pole, lets the boat drift. His eyes settle on Douglass. They are the color of bog peat. "Tell me about slavery."

"What is there to tell?" Douglass says impatiently. He is seated at his desk, endeavoring to compose his memoirs.

"What did you eat?"

"Cornbread. Salt pork. Whatsoever they gave us."

"When you say 'they'?"

Douglass continues scribbling. His plume bobs like a cock's wattle.

"And this talk of corporeal punishment, privations?"

Douglass offers no response.

Lincoln gazes out at the river, at the silvered eddies, and chuckles in a manner he hopes will provoke Douglass's interest. "I am reminded here of the one-legged Paducah planter. It seems he seeded his main acres with orchard rye, hoping to corner the market, leaving only a small patch for cotton. That season an early frost came, and our poor Paducah Joe was left without recourse—"

"Lincoln." Douglass holds his pen aloft. "If you might."

Lincoln gives his long pole a sullen yank.

"I rather like corn bread."

DOUGLASS RETURNS TO the White House. Lincoln has aged a decade. His cheeks look like butcher paper, torn just beneath the eyes. "I have some concerns about the course of the conflict. Your people are not coming to us in the numbers I had hoped, Douglass." His tone is that of a peevish schoolmaster.

"They are trapped, Mr. President. Surely you can see."

"I want you to devise some way to bring them into our lines. Would you do that for me, Douglass? A band of scouts, perhaps?"

"I am hardly the man—"

"We will give you guns, Douglass. And rations and some pay."

"I very much doubt—"

"And morphine, Douglass. Morphine for the injured."

"How is it that you navigate this vessel?" Douglass says.

Lincoln has angled his body against the long pole. With his face upturned, his eyes closed, and the sun beating down, he looks, from this certain angle, like a large, sleepy turtle. "Navigate?" he says.

"Yes. Is there some rudder device, some means of control?"

Lincoln laughs. "The river is like history," he says. "And the flatboat is like a man's life. He can move about in the current, work the pole toward certain intended effects. But he is taken, finally, where the river wishes to take him."

"And where is that, Mr. President?"

"To the sea, Douglass, the deep and final sea."

LINCOLN'S SECRETARY POKES his head in the doorway. "Governor Buckingham of Connecticut," he says.

"Tell Governor Buckingham to wait," Lincoln snaps. "I want to have a long talk with my friend Frederick Douglass."

Douglass blushes. "Really, Mr. President. I am certain the governor—"

"Hush, Douglass. I have no end of Buckinghams. That is why they keep me in this grand house. So the Buckinghams of the world know where to find me. Now then," Lincoln says, "we were discussing scouts. A band of them."

SOUTH OF BURLINGTON, Lincoln purchases a flask of whiskey from a passing gambling barge. Douglass, embarrassed, tries to hide beneath his desk.

"Say, is that Frederick Douglass?"

"No sir." Lincoln moves to shield his companion from view.

"Back away, you oaf. Let me see. But what other man could appear so god-awful? Look at his nose! Like a wedge of moldy cheese. Say there, Frederick!" Others now start to crowd the rail.

"I must ask you gentlemen to cease—"

"Is this your house nigger, Douglass?"

Lincoln steers away from the barge, but a cross flow drags them back.

"And where is Mrs. Douglass?"

"Come dance a waltz, Douglass."

"With your goon here. We've never before seen two niggers dance a waltz."

. . .

DISREGARDING THE ADVICE of his advisors, Lincoln invites a group of rail workers to the White House to celebrate the completion of a line to the Oregon territory. The men move about in rented waistcoats, a sea of nervous mustaches. Lincoln presses the men for accounts of the West. He is fascinated by buffalo, the talk of mountains and endless ridgelines. Long after the men have been marched off, Lincoln can be seen in the West Garden, his arms extended from his body, holding twelve-pound axes in either fist. He looks terribly sad planted there, like a scarecrow trembling in the wind.

LINCOLN DROPS A cube of sugar in the flask and holds it out to Douglass.

"Thank you, no."

"Intemperance does you no favor, friend."

"Still."

"As you wish." Lincoln swallows. "Tell me again about the good widow Glenwood, Douglass. Ah, now there was a woman who knew not to hide from virtue. And its tender erosions. Do not look upon me with such reproach, Douglass. It is not *I* who rhapsodizes my dreams. Also, I have found some sketches among your papers. I did not know you worked on the easel, Douglass."

"I do not."

Lincoln snorts with glee. "Good man! Have a nip!"

Douglass's cheeks redden. "Perhaps just a taste."

Lincoln stands and appears to wobble a bit. He snatches up his stovepipe, turns it onto his head. Sheaves of paper, stashed there with a pair of white kid gloves, flutter about. "What is all this rubbish?"

"You should keep your affairs at the desk," Douglass frets.

"How very important I am!" Lincoln cries, hopping about. "Coded dispatches from the front! Commendation order for one Corporal Bryce Riley! A speech in longhand!"

Douglass picks up the sheet at his feet. "What is this then?"

"How does it go?"

Douglass sniffs the flask and winces another swallow down. He clears his throat and reads: "'It may seem strange that any men should dare to ask a just God's assistance in wringing their bread from the sweat of other men's faces.'"

Lincoln shrugs. "Just a notion I've been playing with."

"Not bad, Lincoln. A bit tentative, perhaps."

Lincoln watches the wind hurl his papers, some landing on the rippled current. Others dance high in the golden noon, as if to drunkenly alight, before tangling in the bank's undergrowth. The merriment drains off Lincoln in dark sheets; his brow collapses. He stoops to collect the floating documents, a motion somber with the weight of undesire.

Douglass, suddenly feeling the effects of drink, improvises an awkward jig. "Cheer up, Lincoln! You are yet the president of these United States!"

Lincoln sucks in his cheeks. "So I am given to understand."

AFTER HE TROUNCES McClellan in the election of 1864, rumors begin to circulate around the capital of a plot to depose Lincoln and appoint a dictator. The president, suffering an intense bout of melancholia, refuses to see members of his cabinet.

"If anyone can do better than me, let him try his hand," he writes, in a note to congressional leaders. "You boys at the other end of the avenue seem to feel my job is sorely desired. Listen: I am but one man in this ruinous union, which has become nothing but a white elephant, impossible to steer or manage."

"AND WHY SUGAR, LINCOLN?"

"The effects of the elixir reach the brain faster."

"It is not just a matter of taste?"

"Certainly not."

"Have you no cause to savor your drink?"

"Of cause I have no end, Douglass. Time—that is the matter."

"Grant makes time."

"He is a soldier. That is his brand."

"And us?"

"We are lovers, Douglass."

DOUGLASS FINDS LINCOLN in his study. The lines along his mouth are sunk deep as runnels. "The speech didn't scour. It was a flat failure. The people are disappointed."

"I thought it a fine speech."

"Everett, Seward, and Lamon all thought it bad. I have blundered, Douglass, and made an enemy of brevity."

"It was succinct."

"No, no, Douglass. You are too kind to me. It was a failure. A perfect failure."

"DO YOU, IN those moments alone, look into the eyes of your wife?"

"That much depends, Lincoln, on whether I am in a position to do so."

Lincoln offers a throaty laugh. His long earlobes, mossed with fine hairs, jiggle. "I see." He plucks at Douglass's silk cravat. "And from whom does this finery derive?"

Douglass displays a band of teeth, fingers the cloth. "This? Hmmmm. Let me see." He tips the flask. "The good widow Winchester, I believe."

"Yes?"

"If memory serves."

"You have had the good fortune of good widows."

"Indeed."

"You have provided them a great comfort, I suppose."

"So I am given to understand."

"I HAVE JUST had the oddest dream," Lincoln says. "Do you remember the flatboat, Mary? Did you know me then? I was there, on the river. The air was like jelly, thick and full of fruit. And do you know what was with me? You will never guess."

Mary does not answer. She is occupied at the task of scratching flowers off the bedside wallpaper with a butter knife.

"I WAS MADE happiest, by jing, at my election as captain of the volunteers in the Blackhawk War."

"You look something like an Indian," Douglass says. "Your cheeks appear chopped at." They are past the Mason-Dixon, floating from St. Louis into Trapville.

"And then my days rail-splitting." Lincoln sips at the flask, wipes his mouth with his wrist, and shambles to his feet. With great ceremony, he spits into one palm, then the other, lifts an invisible hammer over his head, and brings it down onto an equally invisible spike. His height is accentuated by a certain unconsummated grace. "I worked with a fellow named Cooper. His arms were like bolts of pig iron. He celebrated every tie with a song. 'The Sword of Bunker Hill.' 'The Lament of the Irish Immigrant.' Do you know that one, Douglass?"

"No."

Lincoln, still hammering, begins to sing in a reedy baritone:

> *I'm very lonely now, Mary*
> *For the poor make few new friends*

"Will you join me, Douglass?"

"Not just yet, Mr. President."

"We laid track from New Salem to Bedford. In the evenings, Ann would rub my shoulders."

"Ann?"

"With liniment."

"Ann whom?"

Lincoln has sweat through his undershirt. His face is lit with a sudden exhaustion. "Perhaps that is what I meant to remember," he says softly. Lincoln gazes at Douglass for a long while. "They shall set us against one another, friend, we men of honest labor, with our women between us. You do understand that, don't you?"

· · ·

LINCOLN'S FIRST VISION occurs in 1860, following his election as president. He is reclining in his chambers at the Springfield courthouse, facing a looking glass. In this glass he sees two faces at once, both his own. The first is full of a healthful glow. The second reveals a ghostly paleness. He repeats this experiment no fewer than six times. On each occasion, the illusion reappears.

THE FLASK IS DONE at dusk. Both men have stripped down to skivvies. "Honest Abe," Douglass says.

"I cannot tell a lie."

Douglass smiles. "Have you ever kept a pet, Honest Abe?"

"As a lad, I trained a jackrabbit to eat from my hand."

"I should have thought a jackass." Douglass strides to the edge of the flatboat and spits. "Sometimes I dream I am kept as a pet. With many merry widows to feed me carrots and meat and bits of books. My cage is made of woven flax and goldenrod."

"That calls to mind a story, Douglass, of the merchant with a half-wit son. It seems the boy required a sip of molasses before he would to bed each night."

"How has this anything to do with a cage?"

Lincoln frowns. "Yes. I see." Quite independently, the pair dissolve into giggles. "Oh my," Lincoln says.

"Yes?"

"I must relieve myself."

Douglass issues a clarion blare through his fingers: "The business of the presidential bladder must be attended to," he announces. "Please clear a path for the presidential indiscretion."

Lincoln lurches toward the edge of the flatboat. He appears, at best, a man stapled together. "The bank," he says, pawing the air.

"So then, must we by needs speak of the presidential bowels?"

"Stop it now, Douglass. Push on toward the bank."

"Yassah!"

The vessel comes to settle in a stand of reeds. Lincoln tumbles into the water and lets out a whoop. He dogpaddles to the shore, his coarse hair washed off his forehead. Douglass notes the odd shape of his skull, as if someone had pinched him about the jaws and sent the remaining bone ballooning up. He has a small man's face, the eyes of an obedient dog. Lincoln straggles to his feet, britches clinging pinkly to his bottom.

"I am a teapot, Douglass," he hollers. "Here is my spout."

Douglass finds Lincoln alone, reclining on a settee in the West Wing. His eyes are shut, and the puffed flesh beneath them is the color of cherrywood. Douglass retreats to the doorway.

"Don't run off, Douglass," Lincoln says, though his eyes remain shut. "I was just now thinking of you."

"Were you?"

"Indeed. I dreamt us together. You were very brave, Douglass. You tried to save me." Lincoln touches his beard. "Did you know, friend, that I suffer from a kinship with the shades?"

Douglass grins. "Do you?"

"For years, I have known I shall suffer a violent end."

"That is nonsense, sir. You are surely protected."

"I am afraid not, Douglass. That is only a belief to ease the moment. God alone can disarm the cloud of its lightning. Do you agree, Douglass?"

Douglass tries to speak, but his throat constricts, as if clenched by a fist.

Lincoln doesn't seem to notice. "For a man to travel to Africa and rob her of her children—that is worse than murder by my hand. Soon, I believe, the people of the South shall be touched by the better angels of our nature. Consider Goethe: 'Nature cannot but do right eternally.' Are we men not a part of nature?"

"Yes," Douglass says. "On earth and in heaven."

Lincoln opens his eyes and Douglass notes how red they are, like portals of blood. "I am afraid with all my troubles, I shall never get to the place you speak of, friend."

Douglass is halfway returned to New Bedford before he

realizes the source of his disquietude: Lincoln seems to have derived a strange succor from his rumination, as if grief were his only dependable ally.

WHAT SORT OF affiliation is this, Douglass wonders, that seeks to undo a natural repulsion? I do not understand Lincoln, nor he me. We are like two polite giants sharing the same bed and pretending not to mind. Perhaps we are friends because we must not be enemies.

Douglass peers through the telescope he has mounted on a small rise behind the White House. Lincoln is at the window behind his desk, gazing out from the dimmed room. His lips are moving, almost imperceptibly. He looks as if he has been there for years.

"I AM PUBLIC property now," Lincoln tells his marshals. "Open the curtains at once." They are returning to the capital from Antietam by carriage. "I shall not cower in this absurd darkness at the very moment when my behavior should exhibit the utmost dignity and composure."

"Mr. President—"

"Who should want to harm me? This is nonsense."

"But sir—"

"And what if I should die?" he mutters. "Would any of you be so much worse off?"

The marshals part the curtains. Lincoln stares into the night, his beaked profile cast in bronze by the carriage lantern. For the rest of the trip, as the corpses and shanties tumble past, his marshals puzzle over this odd vehemence; whether it is simple pride, willed naïveté, or a variety of reckless self-determination.

LINCOLN AND DOUGLASS lie together, beneath the stars. Without the gas lamps of Washington and New Bedford, the night sky appears far closer.

"Am I so ugly?" Lincoln says.

"I'm afraid so."

"Ape-like? That is what they say, is it not?"

"Only some of them."

"And the others?"

"'Rawboned,'" Douglass says ruefully. "Sometimes 'goonish.'"

"Would you believe that I dreamed to be a stage actor when I was a lad?"

"Or that I dreamed to be a free man?"

"Please," Lincoln murmurs. "Some restraint, Douglass."

"COME AWAY FROM there," Mary says. "What are you looking at? What is it you see in that infernal mirror?"

• • •

DOUGLASS LIES IN the crook of Lincoln's arm. From above, where the night clouds puff like whipping cream, their two forms compose a chain link.

"Tad plays a sort of theater game in his closet," Lincoln says.

"He is your third?"

"Fourth."

"And the others?"

"Eddie died at three. And Willie, Mary's favorite, just last year. Tad will die too, just before his eighteenth birthday. Sometimes, it seems everything I touch dies."

Douglass lays his hand across Lincoln's chest. "I am not dead."

"No. There is that."

"IT SEEMS STRANGE how dreams fill the Bible. I can not say that I believe in them, but I had the other night an episode which has haunted me ever since. Afterwards, I opened the Bible to the 28th chapter of Genesis, Jacob's wonderful dream. I turned to another page, then another, and at every turn encountered some reference to a dream or vision." Lincoln rubs his eyes. "Saul. Nebuchadnezzar."

He is standing at the window behind his desk, facing away from his wife, who has entered in her elaborate bed-clothes.

"Come away from there, Abraham."

Lincoln can see her reflection in the glass, her mouth set in a line.

"Come to bed. You are talking in riddles again."

"Not riddles, dear. Dreams."

"What is the difference?"

Lincoln glances about. The lamps are dimmed, the brownish light best suited to a séance. Stacks of papers rise around him. "Have you noticed how this office has come to resemble a crypt?"

Mary yawns. "If you would simply keep your affairs in order."

PASSING INTO GREENVILLE, Douglass tosses in his bed-clothes. His head aches miserably. Night lends the willows on either bank the appearance of hunched croppers. From behind them, a figure drifts forward, an apparition in gray muslin. Husks of corn lay gnarled in his hair. He stops short of the water, hovering, and moans.

A fury, Douglass thinks. I shall ignore him.

"Yes. I've no business with you, nigger. You are just a fat mouth, a chest full of dull powder. I have come for him. He is mine, now."

"Yours?"

"Surely you don't imagine him to be *yours*?"

The fury opens his black mouth and shivers with laughter.

Douglass shakes Lincoln, thinking to secret him to the other bank. "Lincoln. Arise, Lincoln."

Lincoln lies perfectly still, swaddled in his blanket. The night smells sticky and wrongly sweet.

"Please, Lincoln, arise!"

"ABOUT TEN DAYS ago I retired late, Mary. I was awaiting word from Appomattox. Do you remember the night? I fell into a slumber, standing right here, on this very spot."

"Abraham. Please."

"Soon I began to dream. I felt a deathlike stillness about me. Then I heard subdued sobs, as if a great number of people were mourning. I wandered downstairs. There, the silence was broken by the same sobbing. I went from room to room; no living person was in sight, but the same sounds of distress met me as I passed along. The rooms were lit and every object familiar to me, but where were all the people?"

"I am leaving—"

"I was puzzled and alarmed. I kept on until I arrived at the East Room, which I entered. Before me was a catafalque, on which rested a corpse wrapped in funeral vestments."

"Stop this! I will not hear another word."

Lincoln hears her footsteps retreating.

"Around this corpse were stationed soldiers acting as guards and a throng of people gazing upon the corpse, whose face was covered. Others wept pitifully. 'Who is dead in the White House?' I demanded of one of the soldiers. 'The president' was his answer. 'He was killed by an assassin!' Then came a loud burst of grief from the crowd, which woke me from my dream."

He is still at the window, regarding the night. "Well, it is only a dream, Mary. Let us say no more about it, and try to forget it."

Douglass, perched behind a telescope on his hillside, watches Lincoln's lips, at last, grow still.

THE FLATBOAT GLIDES along toward the Gulf of Mexico. On the far bank, a group of Negroes circles a modest grave. A preacher, his robe frayed and torn, shovels dirt into the pit. A woman cries out. The dawn has made everything wet.

Lincoln climbs groggily to his feet. "My God," he says. "My head feels like a rifle tamped to fire." He rubs his temples and surveys the scene. "Who are they mourning, Douglass?"

Douglass shakes his head.

"Speak man."

"I don't know."

"Perhaps we can offer a prayer." Lincoln directs the flat-boat toward the shore.

"It is too late, sir."

"Have you no compassion, Douglass? Stay a minute and offer condolences. Perhaps the slain—"

"Please, Lincoln, let us pass along."

"They are mourning, friend. We shall exhibit some grace. We must not deaden ourselves to grace."

The preacher pats a final scoop of dirt. The mourners turn, begin to file away from the bier. With a start, Douglass notes a single white face among them: the president's wife, in a plain silk kerchief. Lincoln seems to notice nothing. He presses condolences onto the preacher, whose eyes bug in astonishment.

Returning to the boat, Lincoln draws a breath and slowly exhales. He sets his hand on Douglass's shoulder, steadies himself against a fainting spell. "I am reminded here of a story—"

"Damn you, Lincoln! It is all story with you. Do you not see what is happening?" Douglass shrugs the hand away. He has begun to weep.

Lincoln gazes at the gray morning and lowers himself to a sitting position. His legs dangle, so that his feet are dragged along in the water. To Douglass, they look like a pair of fish struggling exquisitely against the current.

"We are not far from New Orleans," Lincoln says. "We are close now."

"THERE ONCE WAS a man who found no happiness in his life. He was sad every moment of the day. His duties were many and without mercy. Senators ran to him in anger. Common men blackened their hearts on his behalf. A nation of mothers cursed his name. He hoped to make himself content through an adherence to God's will, but when he examined his beliefs found he held none. His wife went insane, Douglass. His children died like flies. His one love perished." Lincoln's voice deepens and curls, assumes the timbre of dream. "He behaved nobly, but for reasons he could not fathom. His faults were but the shadows his virtues cast. He saw himself grimly advancing on history, but came to understand it was the other way around. He grew bored of his own stories and savored none of his achievements. His single respite was sleep. And then that left him too. Hold me, Douglass. All the strange checkered past seems to crowd now upon my mind."

"DO YOU HEAR ME, Mary? I am speaking of a strange dream."

"Damn your dreams. Dress yourself properly. I shan't be made the object of ridicule in a full theater."

"YOU WILL UNDERSTAND," Lincoln says. "You are the one man among all of them who must, by needs, understand." He stares at Douglass and Douglass stares back. Each man can hear the other's breath. They are so close they might embrace.

Instead, Lincoln takes up his long pole and pushes off from the bank. Douglass stands on the shore, watching, until the figure is but a gangly figment, dead to duty, dead to memoranda, dead to the human struggle and to the wickedness of blood, alive only to himself and the green of the gulf.

ON HIS OWN DEATHBED, thirty years later, Douglass will consider a singular vision of Lincoln, his long body laid along the flatboat, his legs dangling, feet cutting through the glassy water, the water washing his glassy feet, the flatboat floating through a city still asleep, floating wakelessly.

THE IDEA OF
MICHAEL JACKSON'S DICK

BRAMBLE WAS TALKING about Michael Jackson again. "What I think he's done is he's bleached his dick. He's tried to turn his dick white."

"You can't turn your dick white," I said.

Bramble poured himself another vodka. "Are you Michael Jackson?" he asked. "If the answer is 'No, I'm not Michael Jackson,' then I don't know why you're talking about his dick."

"*You're* talking about his dick," I said.

"Has he even got a dick?" said Delk.

"Oh, he's got a dick," Bramble said. "He's got a dick alright."

We were on Delk's porch, watching the sun flame out over our neat little southern city, where we'd come to cash in on the emerging field of Cultural Studies. None of us belonged here. That was totally obvious. But they'd let us in and our department chair, being a southerner, was too polite to do the decent thing and rescind our funding.

Every now and again, an undergraduate would stumble past, hungry for some kind of dope. It was a Friday in spring. They were just waiting for sundown to jump on one another.

"You sound pretty confident," I said.

"Photos," Bramble said. "I've seen photos."

"I don't want to hear about this," I said.

"Long and thin and pale." Bramble leered. "Think: albino garter snake."

"How about if we stop talking about Michael Jackson's dick?" I said.

Delk started to sing "Beat It" in a pinched falsetto.

But it was no use trying to stop Bramble. He was like weather in that way—broad and incontrovertible.

"Let me tell you boys a little story. When Jacko was about fifteen years old, he went over to Paris for a special appearance. This was after the Jackson 5 had fizzled out, but before the big solo push. A fallow period, if you will. Anyway, he was over there, when is this, like, late seventies, for a benefit, a benefit for the child victims of land mines."

"Child victims," Delk said. "Perfect."

Bramble waved his cigarette.

"They wheeled all these mangled up kids into this grand ballroom to watch Michael do a little lip-synch and dance thing, these kids from, like, Kurdistan and Latvia, bobbing their heads and blinking at all the flashbulbs from the photographers trying to capture the moment for PR purposes. Suddenly, there's this big commotion at the back of the room. Who should appear but Princess Diana? This is in the early days of the marriage, before the bulimia burned out her throat. She was a huge fan of Jacko. A documented fan. They arranged this backstage meeting, very hush-hush. Michael's kind of shaken up, though, seeing all those kids. He starts to cry. Diana starts to cry. They start talking about all the pressure they have to deal with, you know, being famous, the fans, the press, and so forth. This is what the super famous talk about. It's like their shared story, this aggrandized sense of grief, no one understands. Lady Di is smitten. She gets her security detail to smuggle her upstairs to where he's staying and what happens is, they spend the night together. As in, *together*." Bramble settled back in his chair and took a puff of his cigarette. It was lewd how much he enjoyed smoking.

"That is such fucking bullshit," Delk said.

"Check the files."

Bramble did have files. He had read all the literature on Michael Jackson, the semiotic work out of Berkeley, the race-gender surveys undertaken at Michigan, every one of the 67 unauthorized biographies. He had also amassed an archive of video footage. To Bramble, Michael Jackson marked the apotheosis of psycho-sexual/racial celebrity confusion. He had explained all of this in a lengthy paper (forthcoming in *The International Journal on Pop Culture and Its Discontents*) titled "Pretty Young Thing: The Making of a Post-Modern Frankenstein."

He had no compunction about lying when it came to Jackson either, because Jackson had, in his view, placed himself beyond traditional categories of truth. Whatever vestige of authentic personhood might have existed had long since been scraped away.

"Michael Jackson is over," Delk said. "Nobody gives a shit about him anymore. He was a big deal, like, 20 years ago. *Thriller* and all that. You know who cares about him now? The French. I don't know anyone in the United States who gives a shit about him."

"Why is his trial front-page news?"

Bramble had a point. All week long, the local paper had been running stories about Jackson's lawsuit against his plastic surgeon. They'd run a photo on the front page, showing Jackson swathed in bandages. He looked like a delicate mummy.

"That's just, like, the whole media sell-shit mentality. They put him on TV because he's a freak. There's no deeper meaning," Delk said. "Why do you always assume there's some deeper meaning to Michael Jackson?"

I was afraid Delk might ask this. Bramble took a long, leisurely sip of his vodka. He drank the stuff from plastic bottles, which meant his breath often carried a hint of iso-propyl. I knew this because I lived with Bramble.

"Michael is everything we could ever hope to learn about self-contempt. This is a black man with all the fame and money in the world, a tremendous talent, who despises the conditions of his birthright. So he sets about trying to re-verse all of them. Rather than adult women, he seeks out boys. Rather than accept his masculine Negroid features, he attempts to re-create himself as Elizabeth Taylor from her *National Velvet* days. That's really what he's trying to do. He's even attempted to shave his own bones down. That's why his face is collapsing now. The cartilage is start-ing to poke through. It's a total genetic self-renunciation. When he went to Africa, he wore a mask the entire time. They brought oxygen over there for him, so he wouldn't have to breathe the air. He was scared to breathe the air that other black people breathe."

Delk swigged at his vodka. "RuPaul should beat his ass. I'd pay good money to see that."

"What would be the point?" Bramble said. "Michael al-ready hates himself more than anyone else could."

"Just tell me this," Delk said. "Does he fuck those little boys or what?"

"No no no," Bramble said. "He's scared to death of germs. What he wants, actually, is to be welcomed by these little boys into their world. He's revisiting the trauma of his own boyhood."

"What trauma?" Delk said. "He was a fucking rock star. Or whatever, before that, Motown."

"His dad beat him," Bramble said. "His brothers despised him. His mother was in denial. No one ever made him feel loved as a child. He was just this little performing monkey. It was a kind of slavery. And all the desperation. Do you know where he grew up? Gary, Indiana. Have you guys ever been to Gary? It's a graveyard."

"When were you in Gary?" I said.

"I've driven through," Bramble said. "A couple of times."

There was a nice little silence, which made me hopeful that we could stop talking about Michael Jackson. It was a downer topic, one that made me think of America as a terrible disease.

Living in the South didn't help. Race wasn't something you discussed here, unless you were in a classroom, and most towns were really two towns, the black part and the white part, and people might spend time in the other town (usually blacks who made the trip over for work), but aside from that, no one wanted to mess with the karma. There was too much history, the blood of a native war, and all these elaborate manners had sprung up to make sure the dead stayed buried.

"I'd fuck Janet," Delk said finally.

"I'd fuck Tito," I said. This was not true. I would not fuck Tito. But I was hoping to throw Bramble off the scent.

"What you have to realize about Michael is that he's become dependent on his own mortification. This is what's known as the Fame–Flagellation Nexus. Think of it as a more sophisticated version of the Negative Attention Syndrome. The subject attempts to use an external source of adulation to counteract a sense of worthlessness. This naturally causes an internal conflict, guilt over his success, invariably subconscious, which spurs a set of behaviors aimed at undercutting the adulation. Virtually everything Michael does is engineered to humiliate him. The sham marriages, the shitty records, the bizarre surgeries, the dangling babies—"

"I don't think that monkey did much for him," Delk said.

"Bubbles," Bramble said. "He was a *chimp*."

Bramble had devoted an entire section of his paper to Bubbles. It was called "Bubbles: An Object Lesson in Totemic Identification."

"The point is, the tide of fame turns against him. He becomes the object of derision. But even this, you see, is preferable to his internal state, which is one of abnegation, of deadness. He comes to need the abuse in order to exist. Most celebrities suffer from the same affliction, though you'll notice it's more exaggerated among black men, because they are simultaneously loathed and fetishized by the popular culture. Other examples would include Mike Tyson, O. J. Simpson, and Gary Coleman."

I got up and went around back to take a piss on the fig tree. This was something Delk encouraged. He was a meaty fellow with frat-boy tendencies. How he'd wound up in cultural studies was beyond us. My own theory was that an ex-girlfriend had slipped him some kind of Mickey.

Bramble was still buzzing away. I heard the phrases *freak signifier* and *collateral sexualization*. I heard Bramble lighting up another cigarette. I watched myself pissing on the fig tree and wondered if Bramble would ever shut up.

I liked the guy. He was relentless in a way I admired, and totally, annoyingly earnest. But there was something desperate in his tone, which made me suspect he hadn't really decided who he was, that he hoped all his ideas might make him someone. I'm not saying I was so different; a bit less obvious, maybe.

I zipped up and turned around and was startled to find a little girl, maybe about five, watching me from the second-story window of the house behind Delk's. She hadn't seen anything vital, I was pretty sure. But she knew I'd been taking a piss and that it was probably wrong for an adult to be pissing on a fig tree.

She smiled, like she was a little bit embarrassed, because she herself had been caught doing something naughty before and knew that it felt good, as well as bad.

I waved at her. She lifted one hand from her thigh and returned the wave. Then she did a little pirouette, some kind of ballet move, which made her blond hair float through the air.

I gave her the thumbs-up and she started laughing and ran off.

When I got back to the porch Bramble was all alone.

"Where's Delk?"

"He went inside to make a phone call or something."

"You bored him away," I said. "Seriously. You can't just Michael Jackson people to death."

"He was interested," Bramble said. "He was taking an interest."

"Not really," I said.

Bramble waved his cigarette at me.

The sun was falling away, turning the high clouds pink and orange. It really was a nice city we lived in, very clean, with an excellent park system. You would have never known that people were dying of unhappiness, right there under the nose of God.

"We should get something to eat," I said.

"Did I really bore him?" Bramble seemed to be considering this, turning the question this way and that in his long, yellowed fingers. "Do I bore you, Mikey?"

"It's not a matter of boring," I said. "But sometimes, I don't know, I just wish you'd let old Jacko alone. He seems unhappy enough."

I hadn't meant to say this. I suppose a part of me was jealous of Bramble, of his ability to ignore obvious social cues, his assurance.

"I'm not trying to be a jerk. Geez, Mikey. You're making me feel like a jerk." Bramble polished off his vodka and stood up, a little uncertainly. For a sec, I thought he might start crying, that it would be one of those scenes.

"I just feel like we should be learning something about ourselves when we look at the world," he said.

"You're absolutely right," I said. "Come on, Bram. You know you're my homeslice."

This was what we called one another. It was a way of reassuring ourselves that we weren't alone, a kind of improvised brotherhood. Later, we'd head over to Sully's and sit around the bar and try to figure out what it meant to be an adult, to love ourselves convincingly. It was a constant struggle. I held out my hand and Bramble gave me the old soul clasp.

But there was something somber in the moment that we couldn't undo. It might be said that Bramble had stumbled into his own Fame–Flagellation Nexus. Or that I had spoken a bit too much, turned the truth in a cruel direction. I wanted to apologize.

Before I could do that, though, we heard a wondrous noise, a wall of shimmery notes rising from Delk's ancient stereo, floating out into the dusk. It was all there suddenly, in a way that seemed a small miracle of the heart: the syncopated three-beats, the bubbling bass line, the sunny guitars, and then, just as suddenly, Michael Jackson's tender alto rising up: "Oh baby, give me one more chance!"

Bramble closed his eyes and smiled. He began to move his hips without realizing it. Delk leapt out onto the porch, yowling the chorus at the sweet, terrified vegans across the street. I thought about the little girl I'd seen in the window, how she had offered up her performance to me. It was what children did, naturally—they drew love from the world. And they did so not because they were inherently good and pure, or any of that other Shirley Temple garbage. But just the opposite: because they knew how much the world could hurt them at any time, how quickly the fates could turn, and this made them desperate to charm.

Michael Jackson had felt all this so purely once. His voice had enthralled the world, tamed the horrors he knew would find him, and he kept trying to get back there and he couldn't. But for the rest of us, it was still there, what he'd done. It was A-B-C, easy as 1-2-3. There was no way to resist the joy.

THE PROBLEM OF
HUMAN CONSUMPTION

PAUL, IN THIS CASE, is a widower. His wife died thirteen years ago. He kept their daughter away as much as he could. There were relatives around to play with her, to shower her with gifts and praise. His wife grew pale in the study. Her hair fell out. The disease ate her body in delicate bites. How do you explain such things to a four-year-old?

Paul has not moved or remarried. He has not taken a new job or dated a pretty secretary. To become unstuck has proved more than he can manage. He took his one grand risk of love. He met his desire and clung to her and she dissolved in his arms.

He lives with his daughter in this same house, which is a little too big for the two of them. (There were plans for a second child.) Jess has grown into an awkward beauty. She has a great head of hair, which she wears long down her back. Paul watches her on occasion, speaking to one of her suitors on the phone. She has aspects of her mother, an easy, unexpected laugh, that hair, which trails behind her like the train of a gown. But she is burdened with his bones—stolid, heavy. She dresses to conceal her figure, the broad pallid curves. Her young body swims inside baggy jeans and sweaters.

The moment in question is a Saturday night. Paul is alone in his home. Jess is out on a date, with a boy, or perhaps a group of them all together, at a bowling alley or movie house, chattering about the people they fear they are, or wish to become.

Jess has given herself over to this second life, among her peers, and Paul makes every effort not to hold her back. It is vital that she find happiness where she can.

Paul occupies himself by acquiring expertise: airplanes, butterflies, the history of the labor movement. He reads articles in his study, by the dozens, and sends electronic messages with his new computer. He imagines them flying from his fingertips, lighting the dark circuits of the world with knowledge.

But on this particular evening an ancient restlessness has stirred within Paul and he wanders from the lamps of his study into the kitchen and makes a sandwich. The fridge is divided by shelves, because Jess has decided, of late, to become a vegetarian. He admires this decision. It strikes him as the only sustainable solution to the problem of human consumption. (Six billion mouths to feed. The energy required to raise a calf versus a field of beans. He has studied the problem.) Paul has even considered telling her how much he admires her decision. But this would deprive Jess of the pleasure of her righteousness. And it would expose him as a hypocrite, because meat is one of his few pleasures. He gazes at the items on her shelf—the bumpy soups and mysterious chutneys, a jar of green liquid that appears to be growing spores—and reaches for the smoked ham.

The first sandwich only serves to make him hungrier, so he eats a second. The phone rings and he goes to pick it up, but there's only a dial tone. These hang ups are a new development. They make Paul feel embarrassed, as if Jess is ashamed of him.

He wanders the house, unable to attach himself to a task. He turns on the TV and allows the colors to wash over him for a few minutes. They make his eyes tear up. He doesn't worry about his daughter. There is something ruthless in her sensibility. He pities the boy who mistakes her for an easy mark.

Paul arrives at Jess's room. He's not sure how he got here. A minute ago, he was watching the History Channel—that terrible siege at Leningrad, grown men feeding on the soles of their children's shoes—and now he's standing in his socks before her room. The door is open a crack, because Jess knows her father isn't a spy. He has always kept himself from such obvious curiosities.

Her room is much larger than most of her friends', because, in fact, he's given her the room that once served as the master bedroom. He sleeps downstairs, in the room that used to be his study. And his study is the room that she slept in as a child. All these changes were made hastily, after the funeral, and they never seemed unnatural to him. Jess has always required more room.

As it is, she's expanded her possessions to fill the space. She has a set of drums in one corner, which she rarely plays anymore, thank God. There are two desks, one devoted to her schoolwork, the second to her recent fanatical interest in astrology. There are a few sweaters on the bed, which is half-made, and a stack of books on her nightstand, all devoted to astrology.

The room is warm, unexpectedly so, and filled with the sweet, slightly burned residue of sandalwood incense. Paul turns this way and that. He lopes into Jess's bathroom and pees and wipes the rim and stares at the bulky makeup bag beside the sink, afraid to touch it. He walks back into her room and glances at the possessions on her dresser—an ivory chopstick, a tube of something called Spirit Gel, a tiny tin of breath mints—strange relics of her personhood scattered in the low light.

There is another object there, glimmering beneath a pile of scrunchies. Paul doesn't want to disturb the pile. He doesn't want to snoop. But he does want to know what might be glimmering, so he turns on the light and peers into the pile. The object is his wife's wedding band.

Paul's reaction is one of terror. He hurries over to turn off the light and sits on the edge of the bed and his heart is galloping. He has always assumed his wife was buried with her ring. He has an image of her laid out, the slender gold band on her finger. This is ridiculous, though, because she insisted that her body be used for medical research, and they didn't bury her at all. There had been a memorial service.

He tries to remember the last time he saw his wife, but cannot. He remembers only the rails of the bed, the steel of them, and the humiliating smell of decay. At some point, she must have given Jess the ring. But why had she done this? And how had Jess managed to keep this from him? And why? Was this a secret between the two of them? And if so, what was the ring doing on her dresser, left out like a bit of costume jewelry?

These are the mysteries that consume him as he sits on his daughter's bed with his hands in his lap. They matter as much as any of the others, the fact that people die for no good reason, that they choose to hate when love becomes unbearable, that a certain part of them, starved of happiness, gives up, shuts down, goes into hiding.

Paul can feel the squeeze of panic in his chest. He has worked so hard to avoid the traps of mourning, the self-pity and rage. He has made sure his daughter feels loved. He has given her all the gifts of compassion she will bear. But this ring, it feels like a betrayal.

He wants to leave her room, shut the door, drift back to his study. Instead, he gets up and walks to the dresser and stares at the ring. He removes the scrunchies one by one, with the chopstick. He picks the ring up and puts it down and picks it up again and it's heavier than he expected or denser or something and he notices a hair, a single strand of his daughter's hair, clinging to metal. The hair is looped through the band, actually, in such a way that when he holds both ends the ring is suspended. He lifts one end and then the other and the ring slides back and forth and this simple motion, in the somber light of the room, strikes him as miraculous: the ring is defying the law of gravity.

It is at this precise moment that his daughter appears in the doorway. She often finds her father asleep at this hour, in the chair in his study. The habit has become a joke between them. He denies in mock indignation, she gently accedes. *Whatever you say, Dad.*

Jess is in the doorway for a second before her father realizes she's there, and for a portion of that second she's not even entirely sure what she's seeing—a stranger in her room, a thief, should she be frightened?—but then she recognizes his socks and the bedraggled clumps of the hair above his ears, which she has always wanted to trim.

She sees that he is hunched over something shiny and that this shiny thing is sliding back and forth, between her father's fingers. There is an instant, the tiniest of instants, in which she too believes the object is floating in the air, and this possibility of magic is a thread that connects them.

Then she sees that the object is the ring, her mother's ring, and she is furious at herself for being so careless and a little frightened of what her father might do, and a little frightened, also, of what her father might not do, that he may be too cautious at this point to express what she would consider an appropriate rage. Because she did not, after all, receive this ring from her mother. She stole the ring from her father, from a shoe box tucked away on a high shelf in the closet in his study, where it was stashed, along with the results of a blood test and a yellowed marriage license and a ribbon which she imagines her mother wore on her wedding day, though she has never been able to find it in the photos.

Jess is considering all this when her father looks up.

Remember: the light is low. It is difficult to read precise expressions. These two are, more than anything, familiar shapes in the dark.

Paul feels dizzy with shame. He has been caught in his daughter's room, playing with his wife's ring, a ring which now belongs to Jess. The transfer of this object between the two women is, in his mind, an ancient secret he had no business discovering. He wishes he had slipped away a few minutes earlier, as he intended.

Jess doesn't say anything. She is capable of excruciating silences. She doesn't quite know how she should react, though she does have a vague sense that her father should take the lead here; he is the adult and the rightful owner of the ring and the person whose actions have initiated the moment.

But her father is standing there, frozen. The ring is quivering. Jess waits for him to speak. She still hasn't figured out exactly how the ring is able to float there between his fingers. She wants to switch on the light, solve the mystery, confess to her secret theft, get everything out into the open. And then again, she wants to back away quietly and run to where her friends are waiting in a car by the curb. Her father might never say anything. He might suppose he had dreamed the entire thing. She would not put that past him.

Paul looks at his daughter, looks her flush in the face, that soft pink swirl of youth, and suddenly he is hungry again, famished. He wants to prepare himself another sandwich, heavy on the ham, and settle into his sleeping chair. But his legs won't move and he remembers, rather too suddenly, that he used to feel this same way after making love to his wife, a queer, short-lived paralysis which overtook him as he lay in a pool of his own heat.

Jess sees her father begin to smile and she takes this as a

bad sign. He looks a bit touched, and this worries her and this worry causes her to take a step into the room. Not a whole step, just an experimental little half-step, as if testing the temperature of a bath.

"Dad?" she says. "Are you alright?"

He nods, or tries to nod. She can't tell.

"Is something the matter?" Jess steps closer. "What's going on?"

Paul is shaking a little. He is looking at his daughter and smelling the sandalwood and remembering a trip they took years ago to the beach, to San Gregorio, south of Half Moon Bay, remembering the sandy hollow where they built a fire to roast hot dogs and marshmallows. He is thinking of his wife, who was not ill yet, not diagnosed, though she was tired more than usual, and despite this, the cooling breeze off the water and the rhythm of surf made them both amorous. Jess was there, too, in a little white bikini which she quickly shed. She ran about naked, chasing the gulls all the way down to the shore, until Paul was forced to go after her. He picked her up and swung her so that her toes swept across the water and she shrieked. The sun beat down on both of them. Later, her mother combed out her hair until she grew drowsy enough for a nap. Paul ate the last of the hot dogs and his wife lay beside him and set her hand on his chest and they whispered to one another, *Should we? Do you think?* though they already were (beneath their blanket) engaged in the soft panic of love. It was a weekday afternoon. There was no one else around. Their daughter slept beside them. Her hair, still blond, fell across her small brown shoulders.

Jess is still calling his name and she has, by now, stepped close, close enough to smell the meat on his breath, the tang of mustard, and she, too, is thinking about that trip to the beach, though she isn't quite certain where she was, only that it was someplace outdoors that smelled of fire and smoked meat and that she woke to find her father on top of her mother, moving against her with a wet desperation, as if to devour her, while her mother smiled delicately in profile. Then her father looked over and saw her watching and seemed to want to say something to her, to yell or apologize, she couldn't tell which, and she shut her eyes and turned the other way and soon after her mother got skinnier and skinnier and they locked her in the study. This is when all the aunts began to arrive and to give Jess gifts, one every morning. They told her she was beautiful again and again.

Jess would have no idea, at this point in her life, that she has associated this memory with her mother's death, that, in some hidden cavern of her heart, she regards her father as having killed her mother, or, more precisely, that she regards she and her father as having collaborated in the murder of her mother.

She knows only that she has arrived home to find her father in her room, that he is shaking, his eyes clouded over, and because she loves her father she moves to embrace him, not a full hug, just a brushing of their two bodies in the dark. Her hair is shining like some wild flag and he is staring down at the ring, breathing heavily.

Paul is so hungry now he could eat a pig, a cow, an entire farm of useless beasts. All the fields of crops in all the countries of the world would not fill his belly. He can smell the smoke of the fire and the meat and he is lying with his wife on the warm sand and he is holding on to his only given daughter and he is starving to death.

It is important to remember that this is only a single moment, this tentative caress, nothing they will speak of again, an *interlude*.

It is important to remember that their crimes are not really crimes. They are simple human failings, distortions of memory, the cruel math of fractured hopes. The only true crime here is one of omission. The woman they both loved has been omitted from their lives. She is a beautiful ghost, a floating ring.

In less than a second, a horn will sound from below. Jess will fall back, swing herself away from her father and toward the rest of her life, her friends waiting in a car by the curb, the night to come, the boy who has told her she is beautiful, who will, in a few hours, in the basement of another home, slip his hand inside her pants and whisper again that she is beautiful.

As for the ring, it will be replaced, first by Paul, on the dresser, under the scrunchies, then by Jess, in the box on the shelf in her father's closet.

Paul will return to the kitchen and make himself a sandwich, but the meat will taste rotten and this taste will haunt his tongue, even after he rinses with mouthwash, and he will drink warm milk instead and take a sleeping pill, and then a second, until he can feel the convincing blur of his dreams. In the days to follow, he will swear off meat, a gradual transition, so as not to detect the notice of his daughter.

But this, of course, is what lies ahead for them, as they race away from the hot center of themselves. Decent lives. Reasonable consumption.

For now, they are still together. Her arms are around him, one hand on his shoulder, the other touching the padding of his waist. He is staring at the ring. Hunger is surging inside him as he sways with her, once, through the dimness of the room. What are they doing here, exactly? Who can say about such things? They are weeping. They are dancing. They are prisoners of this moment and wonderfully, terribly alive.

WIRED FOR LIFE

Janie met the electrician Charlie Song in August. The AC adapter to her laptop had frayed and the connection kept failing. Thus she was forced to jiggle the plug until the current returned, at which point she would have to remain *very still* for many minutes at a time—she worked with the laptop on her actual lap, which was ridiculous, pathetic, but there you have it—lest the sadistic plug icon disappear and the machine revert to battery mode, which was supposed to last six hours but which ran down (and this Janie had timed) in seventeen and a half minutes. It was a little like being a hostage.

Charlie Song's shop was on a stretch of Mass Avenue that was constantly being torn up. Great chunks of asphalt lay about, while men in hard hats and dirty shirts murmured into cell phones. They were hostages, too, though they seemed somewhat liberated by their proximity to loud and senseless destruction.

Inside the shop, dozen of computers had been disemboweled. The remains were so: dusty circuit boards, magnets, stripped screws, woofers like little black eggcups. Keyboards dangled from their cords. Had Torquemada worked in the high-tech medium, this would have been his style.

From the back of the shop, Charlie Song emerged, weaving through the lifeless monitors. He was middle-aged, the color of a weak varnish. He smiled, shyly, as if embarrassed by the size of his teeth.

You need help?

Janie said yes and began to explain her situation, rather too elaborately, while Charlie Song nodded and blinked.

Power broke?

Right, Janie said.

Charlie played the plug between the tips of his fingers. He licked his lips.

Okay. We try. Thursday.

Oh no, Janie said. I mean, if there's any possible way, see, all my work is on the computer, I'm a designer and I've got these projects, deadlines, so if there's any way, I could even wait—

Charlie nodded. It was a complex nod, one that seemed utterly to dismiss Janie's words and yet somehow (was it the mournful aversion of his eyes, the slightly injured stoop?) acknowledged the panic behind them. He carried the adapter to his worktable.

A pair of pliers appeared in his hand. With these he

snipped the cord and peeled back the black casing to expose the wires. The spot where the connection had frayed looked like a tiny copper fright wig. Charlie gazed at it and let out a sigh and played at the filaments with his thumb. Then he clicked on the ancient contraption at the center of his table, something like a whisk.

Is that a welder? Janie said.

Charlie Song said, Sadder.

Sadder?

Sadder. Sadder gun.

Janie wanted to ask him what did he mean, sadder gun. She had heard of a warm gun, a gatling gun, even a love gun—and now she thought of Drew, her beautiful boyfriend, whose beautiful love gun she would not be sucking this evening, nor receiving inside her with delicious slow-and-hurried difficulty, but which would, instead, lie tremendous and pink across his thigh while she quietly pleasured herself and wept, there in the dark, quietly. Charlie pulled a spool of silver thread from his desk drawer. The label read: SOLDER.

He grazed the shaft of the gun against an old sponge, producing a faint hiss. The tip came against the thread and the solder dissolved into a shiny glob and released a coil of white smoke. Charlie touched at the glob with great tenderness. It was a tricky business, coaxing the wet solder into the space where the wires had come apart. The muscles between his knuckles tensed. His tongue dabbed, a bit rak-ishly, at his upper lip.

Janie felt she should use the occasion to learn a new skill. She might even fix her own adapter the next time it broke. But there was something else. It dawned on her, as Charlie gently replaced the solder gun in its holster and pressed the fused wires to the ohmmeter and watched the needles happily bounce, she was, how to put this, well, there was no other way—the flush of blood, the sudden moist warmth and down-below pulse—turned on.

He was so precise, Janie said. Like a surgeon.

Drew nodded. Isn't it amazing, he said, how hypnotiz-ing the simplest repetitive motions can be? I used to watch my grandpa whittle for hours.

He took a bite of fried dumpling and Janie gazed at his glistening lips, the boyish enthusiasm of his chewing, and at his sideburns, which she'd had to beg him to grow out. They looked devastating.

Yeah, it was like he had this touch, you know. Janie paused. Almost like a sensual thing.

She wanted to elaborate, wanted this terribly, but Drew had stopped chewing and his eyes began to narrow and she knew that anything more she said would be construed as an *unacknowledged, passive-aggressive* attack because Drew didn't happen to feel comfortable, for now, expressing himself physically. Or, as Janie sometimes put it, after a glass of wine with friends: *he refuses to fuck me.*

Three years ago, when she and Drew met, this had not been an issue. They'd had sex then, not as much as she would have liked (never as much as she would have liked), but she felt this was somehow only fair because he was so beautiful after all, even his cock was beautiful, venous, unwavering, with its soft swollen head like an Italian plum, and she so thrilled to the music of his body and the sweet painful inconvenience of love between them, and told herself that such gifts were not to be gone at greedily. He was a good lover, too, generous in the modern fashion, determined to bring her off, though he tended to shy from his own pleasure.

All of which memorialized the occasions when he did come, when he would let her suck or stroke to the end, the prodigious and sticky end, which wrenched him free of his poise and brought the blood to his skin and the ooze of him down her chin or thighs and the final shuddering. He held her so violently in these moments she felt sure he would crush her ribs, that they would perish together, ecstatic and doomed.

Drew was starting in on the cashew chicken, asking her if she wanted green tea. It's good for the lymphatic system, he said, gesturing with the pot. His eyes were so lambent Janie wanted to poke one with a chopstick.

Whatever it was, the danger of vulnerability, some past trauma, a chemical deficit—*whatever*—the sex had diminished. He had grown more and more uncomfortable with contact, until she wasn't allowed to touch him in suggestive places at all; his body would go cold. She finally convinced him to attend couples therapy with Dr. Dumas, who spoke with great fluency about libido dynamics and intimacy paradigms and asked them to engage in tummy therapy (*circle the lower abdomen, please, with just the tips of the thumbs*) a ritual they both considered so humiliating that they had agreed, without actually discussing the matter, to stop seeing her.

Now Janie worried this topic, the Drew-won't-touch-me-fuck-me topic, all the time, on the phone, to her friends, and when she hung up, the cuff of her ear hurt. They always told her the same thing: *get out, get out, get out,* or, *have an affair, call an old boyfriend, that one who used to play in the new-wave band, just to see, you've got to.* They pleaded with her, keened at her, and she agreed with them, made little vows and planned her speech. But then she would actually see Drew, the cleft in his chin and the long, elegant hands, and this would completely fuck her up.

She was becoming a person she hated.

Besides, her friends, with their chintzy Cosmo-girl-empowerment shtick—she had seen them in Drew's presence, the way they fussed and preened and found excuses to touch him. *Is that a new watch? I never noticed that freckle.* Once she had walked in on a scene in which Margo and Ali seemed to be asking Drew if he had ever seen their nipples, and would he like to, a charge they denied with much forced laughter.

Janie was a set designer. It was her job to make things look perfect, and that was at least part of the problem. Drew looked perfect. When they entered a party, there was always a fleeting hush, a flurry of swung necks and murmurs.

On Sunday mornings, he sat in the bay window with his tea and his cat, a stray he had named Clawed Rains, and the sun scrolled down the side of his face and Janie tried to determine if she would still love him if she were blind and the answer was, well, she was pretty sure. Drew was funny and self-deprecating and he could dance, he was graceful. (Often, as she set about a new design, she would envision Drew waltzing her under the houselights.) There was a decency about him. He designed curricula for at-risk kids, a little tiresome on the subject, yes, but *committed.* Noble.

But the point, the point, she wasn't blind, thank God, and oh dear God, he was good-looking. He was another species. He was Elvis, Elvis in his soldier days, with the Egyptian profile and the crew cut, only Drew was pale and something Janie wanted to call ruddy, kind of pink and splotched, which sounded bad, but on him, on his particular person, his face, and the veins that stood out on his inner arms and his calves and his ruddy, muscled ass . . .

He was Scottish. Andrew Coletart, Drew. His people were ugly people, the Coletarts, mule-faced and benevolent. Every time Janie looked at Mrs. Coletart (whom she privately thought of as Mrs. Muletart) she thought: How could this be? How could this creature have sprung from your loins?

This was how she managed the whole affair: she relied on her own shame, her inexhaustible shame, and converted his rejection into something bearable by assuming she was at fault, that she pushed too hard for his love or wasn't pretty enough for him or smelled funny. He had asked her once why she didn't wear perfume more and now she was convinced she smelled funny, funny down there, and washed obsessively and even douched, and it was odd, really, because her old boyfriend, not the new-wave bassist, but the one who taught preschool and whose fingers smelled of paste, he had told her how good she tasted, like the juice of tulips, and insisted that she taste herself on his tongue and yeah, it was hokey—the juice of tulips, *Christ*—but every time he said it she felt a damp surge.

Drew had cleared the dishes and set a bowl of ice cream down in front of her. It looked like a lump of wet rust. Red bean, he said helpfully. He was into themed meals. Do you want hot fudge, babe? I can heat some.

Janie knew somewhere inside her that Drew loathed himself or didn't really love her enough or was gay *(themed meals?)*. But this part of her remained unconnected to the other part, which gazed at him, in his beauty and bearable kindness and told herself to settle down if he didn't want to do it for a while and quit being such a trollop.

In October, the adapter began fritzing out again. Janie spent a week jiggling the cord and remaining frozen, until some motion, a tick, a yawn, a sneeze, would cut the connection and she would curse very quietly, or sometimes louder, and once she even shoved Clawed Rains hard enough to send him thudding against the entertainment center.

Back she went to Charlie Song, but she arrived too early and had to stand on the sidewalk and watch the road crew, still joyously ripping up the street. One of the men straddled a jackhammer and flipped a switch and suddenly the blade bit into the asphalt and the great tool sent violent shudderings through his body.

Charlie Song appeared a few minutes later, short and disheveled in the clattering sun. Wisps of black hair lay across his scalp. The flesh around his mouth was finely creased. He was nonplussed to find Janie waiting for him and entered the shop with his hands brushing the air before him, as if to clear away cobwebs.

Janie pulled out the adapter and Charlie began his nimble inspection; his eyes looked pained at the state of the cord, whitish at the rim of the coupler, like old licorice.

How you hold? You use rough?

Janie said, No.

Charlie squinted. You hold funny?

Well of course she did hold the machine funny, and this did lead, rather directly, to a severe bending of the cord. But she saw no reason to confess all this to Charlie Song.

The receipt says your work is under warranty, she said.

At the word *warranty,* Charlie shied away. His eyes welled into little pools of sullenness.

October, he said.

Janie nudged her boobs against the glass counter. The receipt says 90 days.

Charlie smiled miserably. He did not look at Janie, nor especially at her boobs, but carried the adapter with its cord dragging behind and set it down on his worktable and disappeared into the back of the shop. He returned with his spool of solder and hunkered down before his sadder gun while Janie pretended not to notice. There was a delicious, excruciating aspect to the tableau.

The components in Charlie's shop seemed now to be replicating: resistors and volt relays and hard drives in their shiny silver antimagnetized baggies and tangles of taffy-colored wire. The display rack nearest the door was stuffed with CD-ROMs covered in—Janie was almost sure of this—bird shit. On one shelf sat a small portable TV monitor. There, in the watery green light, was a man hunched over a desk, with a young woman looming over him. It took a moment for Janie to realize she was being filmed.

Charlie Song worked intently. He snipped the coupler and stripped the wires and his hands, his nicked, runty hands, moved with an extraordinary attention that seemed to Janie the most obvious and overlooked aspect of love. Charlie peered down at the thin silver bridge he had installed. The fissure was barely visible, but it was there, enough to cut the current. He let his fingertip linger on the spot.

On went the sadder gun and Charlie jumped up from his desk. He returned a few moments later with a jar of water, into which he dipped the old sponge, and quite suddenly there was music in the shop as well, a Bach fugue, a mournful drift of violins, and Charlie dabbed the gun against the sponge and gathered solder at the tip and Janie felt a sudden trill in the place where her thighs met. She understood now what they had been up to earlier: a kind of spat, a kind of foreplay. Coils of smoke rose up from the dissolving solder. Charlie sneezed, delicately, three times in a row. Janie had to restrain herself from touching his cheek.

· · ·

THAT NIGHT SHE went back on the promise she had made to herself, which was not to touch Drew till Halloween, nor to entice or seduce or cajole, but to let him come to her. Earlier, at Taco Loco, Drew drank not one, but two beers, and his mood had been buoyant as he discussed a new funding source for his truancy seminar. She was preoccupied by his breath, its bouquet of yeast and poblano chiles.

Now she slipped into bed in her camisole and reached out to touch the muscles along his spine. She was careful not to linger, to carry on her chatter, and Drew listened to her and did not tense up and he smelled sweet and gamy and his hair was just oily enough to shine in the dull light from the alley and he had, after all, drunk that second beer, so she let her hand slip down his back, then lip beneath the band of his boxers, at which point Drew murmured, Do you want to cuddle?

This was his new ploy: cuddling.

It technically fulfilled the requirements of affection while providing none of the actual benefits. For Drew, cuddling meant she could spoon him, or he could spoon her, but if certain unspoken boundaries were crossed—say, playing with his earlobe, or making a sudden grab for his scrotum—then this was no longer cuddling but had become *pressure*, which was bad, oh very bad that pressure, the source of all their problems. It caused Drew to tense

and begin speaking as if he were addressing a grant com-
mittee.

Still, she took the offer to cuddle. She took it and wrapped
her body around his and stroked his shoulders in a manner
she hoped would be deemed innocuous while simultaneously triggering the elusive chain reaction that would wake
the blood within him. She hugged Drew from behind.
Her pubic bone, her poor, neglected pubic bone, pressed
against his tailbone. His hair smelled like an herb garden.
She kissed the back of his neck and let her lips linger until
she felt the shifting muscles. He was turned on. At last, he
wanted her and she reached for him, tugged at his hipbone,
and the straps of her camisole slipped free and her fingers
skimmed his belly on the way down. But suddenly something clamped onto her wrist and she heard Drew say,
Damn it.

His body was a pale outline in the dark.

We talked about this, he said.

Get away, Janie said, sobbing a little.

Which he did, of course, the clever bastard, and slept on
the couch and in the morning sent Clawed Rains in as an
emissary. Then he brought her breakfast on a tray.

I don't want breakfast, Janie said.

What do you want? he said.

She tipped the tray and watched skim milk soak her big
stupid tits.

Why are you doing this to me?

Drew sat on the edge of the bed and took her hand.

I don't know, he said quietly.

Are we ever going to touch again?

Give me time, Janie. I'm going through some changes.

What sort of changes? The sort that involve wanting to have sex with men?

Drew ran a hand through his hair, which still smelled like herbs. No, Janie. Nothing like that. I just don't feel . . . He mumbled a word that sounded like *sassy*.

You don't feel sassy? Is that what you said?

Sexy, Drew said. He rubbed his face with his hands. I don't feel sexy.

Janie wanted very much to laugh. She wanted both to laugh and to run her tongue along the rim of his nostrils, which were flaring deliciously.

Is this some kind of joke, she said. Not sexy? You can't possibly, do you have any idea, my God, you are one of the most, honey, look in the mirror.

Drew shrugged. I just don't feel it.

Well then let me feel it. I can prove it to you. She reached for his shoulder. We can take care of this right now. *Please.*

Drew refused to look at her. Instead, he began setting the overturned dishes back on the tray. That's not how it works, honey. You have to feel it from the inside.

Janie wanted to tell him: No no. Wrong! That *is* how it

works. Our sense of beauty comes from outside, from the world. We aren't born feeling desirable, you lummox. Please. Let me help you.

But his shoulder had gone dead under her touch and now he was flashing her his adorable sulky underlip and asking: Can't we just cuddle? Please, baby. Don't give up on me. I'll get it back.

JANIE WOULD REALIZE only later that she had provoked the third visit to Charlie Song. It was the holiday season, which meant naked trees and slush and a walloping case of seasonal affective disorder. She'd taken Drew to visit her folks for Christmas, which was really two trips, one to the Mother, the other to the Father, who, though technically cohabitating, lived on separate floors of a camp house on Squam Lake and did not, as a rule, speak.

Her mother had survived cancer, but the dark fog of decay had left her prone to eccentricity. She tottered down the shore flanked by her Shih Tzus, cussing at the speedboats. She despaired of the rustling spruce. Winter had flayed the mountains around the lake and layered the roads with mulch. The silver bass slept in beds of frozen mud.

Drew was magnificent. He chopped wood and beat hoarfrost off the granite shingles and helped her father manage the terrifying new gas heater. He lumbered about in a mackinaw and a stocking cap with a look of dumb radiant industry. Her mother and father adored Drew. They gazed at him with abject lust and competed for his attention and seemed to regard Janie as the lucky but not-quite-appreciative-enough recipient of a Lotto jackpot. They made loud dithering comments about future family vacations. Eagerly, creepily, they transitioned from potential in-laws to groupies.

On the day after Christmas, Janie woke to the whinny of floorboards. The Mother laughed like a loon, delirious, absurd. Janie assumed she was being tossed by dreams. But then the Father produced a groan and the song of bedsprings began and Janie decided she might just puke, that puking would certainly be justified in this instance. Drew lay on his back. His face was puffed a bit and softened around the cheekbones. She peeled back the comforter and watched his peaceful breathing. She imagined him flouncing through the Scottish Highlands in a kilt, with nothing underneath, letting the fields of heather fan across his lovely, pointless boner. Then she started packing.

Back in their apartment, Janie drank vodka tonics and tried not to cry. Clawed Raines mewed for attention and slid his gray gums along her knuckles. Janie tossed him away. But Clawed jumped back up and began to knead her lonesome boobs and rather than comforting her, this persistence made Janie furious and she flicked the cat, hard, with her index finger, right on his spongy little snout, which caused him to sneeze convulsively and this caused Janie to weep convulsively and it began to snow outside and the wind howled and the phone rang and rang. She yanked at the coupler that attached the adapter to her laptop viciously, rhythmically, while she made her choked little human sounds, until she felt the coupler snap.

Charlie's shop was warm and cluttered. It smelled of cherry syrup or burned rubber, perhaps both. The man who appeared from in back was not Charlie Song, but a younger, stockier fellow with an optimistic expression, which Janie immediately resented. He spoke an earnest, hollow brand of English, customer servicese.

Where's Charlie? Janie said. Who are you?

It occurred to her that she had had too much to drink, though she was, pleasantly, drunk enough to forgive this perception.

The young man pushed up his spectacles. Charlie's gone. May I help you with something?

What do you mean *gone?* Janie said. What does *gone* mean?

He's running an errand. My name is Fred Lui. I'm his associate. Perhaps I can help you with something?

This is sort of a personal problem, Janie said.

Fred cocked his head. Are you alright? he said.

Of course I'm alright. What sort of question is that? I just need a repair done and Charlie is the one who's done it previously, twice previously, and he asked me specifically, if I needed further assistance, as I understood the arrangement, I was to see him. *Okay?*

Fred held up his hands, as if he were being robbed. Okay, he said.

So Janie sat down amid the dingy keyboards and casings and springs and watched the snow fall on the road crew, who had constructed, by this time, a small crater. The TV monitor was still on the shelf and she glanced a few times at the tiny chlorophylled world which was her world, in which she was tucked, pretty and sad, in a far corner.

It was past five when Charlie appeared and immediately Fred rose from behind the counter and began to speak to him in Chinese—she guessed it was Chinese—and Charlie Song looked utterly ruined, with red bags under his eyes and his worn-out teeth.

Charlie, she said.

He was wearing a cap, some kind of foolish brimmed cap, and when he pulled it off his hair rose up in black clefs.

Problem again? Why problem? I made good repair last time.

Janie straightened the hem of her dress. Yes. Of course you did. Charlie, please. It was my fault. I dropped the machine.

No warranty, Charlie said.

The flecks of snow on his coat had begun to soak through. Janie wanted to throw a shawl over his shoulders.

I was hoping we might discuss this—alone.

Charlie began shaking his head. No. No fix now. Very busy. You come back. January.

But Charlie, you know, I wouldn't ask unless it was an emergency. I'll pay you. I can pay in cash. Janie took a step closer and Charlie backed against the counter.

Holiday, he said.

Janie took another step forward, but Charlie ducked left, toward the back room, all the while shaking his head and saying: Comp USA. They have good technician there.

Please, Janie said. This won't take long.

She began, then, to chase him, around the counter and through the thickets of zip drives and modems. Please. Charlie. Let's not be like this. I just need you—

Something caught in her throat. She was certain her face was a shiny and lurid thing. She'd put on lipstick and too much mascara and she was wearing a gown, a fucking evening gown. The adapter was clutched to her bosom.

Fred looked on, mortified.

But Charlie, who was backed against a door that read EMPLOYE ONY, with his hand on the knob, peered at Janie for a long moment. It was not a look of pity, exactly, but of some larger human recognition. Charlie scratched his nose and glanced at the floor. He muttered a few words to Fred in Chinese.

Okay, he said to Janie. We do. But last time. Last time.

Of course, Janie said.

Fred muttered something plainly disapproving and put his windbreaker on and marched out of the shop. The two of them were, at last, alone.

Charlie went to his desk and stripped the wires and fired up his sadder gun and the snow continued to fall. Outside, the workers lumbered home and the air above the road took on a metallic shimmer and Charlie twisted the strands of wire and soldered them to the bridge. Janie pulled up a stool and watched him.

Can we listen to music? she said.

Charlie shrugged. He seemed to recognize that something deeply unorthodox was transpiring and ducked into the back room; a few moments later Bach filled the store.

Janie did not speak as he worked, but she imagined what Charlie's life might have been like, how he came to this country on a boat, probably a very small boat, or else wedged down at the bottom of a very large boat, and how he had struggled to open his own shop and now sent money back to his family in a place like Kunming or Shenyang and how his wife had died, oh his poor wife, and this had left Charlie Song as a widower and he lived in a small apartment with very few windows and had to cook for himself and sublimated all of his erotic impulses into his stunning repairs of RAM drives and disk defragmenters.

And this life, for such a considerate man, this made Janie quite sad, for the alcohol inside her had begun to fade and left a yearning behind. Charlie was touching the wires to the ohmmeter; he didn't notice Janie's tears. She sniffed finally, and he looked up in alarm.

No cry, he said. We fix. Make good connection.

He began searching the drawers of his desk and the countertop and glancing back at Janie and he was a good man, an ugly man, true, but nothing a little dental work couldn't fix. Or maybe she would leave the teeth be. They gave him character.

Charlie returned, cradling something in his palm.

New coupler, he said. Flexible. He pressed the device with his thumb. Now you wired for life. No cry.

Janie's heart began to jump and she set her hand on Charlie's cuff and he stared down at this hand while, with her other hand, Janie grazed his brow and brought her face close to his. She scooted her stool forward and took a lavish breath. Charlie remained very still, like a squirrel. The sadder gun was smoking and Janie thought for a second about Drew and his beautiful bum and imagined the terrible joy she might feel in soldering his hairless cleft shut, though you couldn't really do that, could you?

Charlie was not moving.

Do you like me? Janie said. I like you, Charlie. Do you understand?

She felt the tremors in his arms.

Pretty. Very pretty lady.

Would you like to touch me? I'd like that. If you'd touch me.

Charlie swallowed. His throat revealed an immense suffering.

Married, he said. I have wife already.

Where, Charlie? Is your wife here?

No. Home. Wife home.

He leaned back, but Janie leaned forward and pressed her bundled breasts against him. Her hand settled onto his thigh and this too was shuddering and she set her lips against the damp skin of his temples, which smelled of burned solder, and then he was letting out sad little barks, and saying, Please, pretty lady, please no do that, in a tone of terrible confusion.

Now Janie saw what she had done and took her hands off him and she began to weep again. They were both there, on the green monitor, weeping.

I'm sorry, Janie said. I'm so sorry. I thought—my God, I've been so stupid.

Charlie Song could not stop weeping. His tools were all around him and his hands were at a loss.

I'm sorry, Janie said again. I had no right. Please. Will you forgive me?

Charlie took a minute to settle himself. He wiped at his eyes furiously, as if they were to blame. Then he did something quite wonderful: he gave Janie a gentle little touch, just the tap of a single finger on the back of her hand, or not so much a tap as a stroke, a soft little accidental stroke, in the hopes that she would stop crying, and he said, Pretty lady, pretty lady, don't cry. I fix. Promise. Promise.

There was an electricity to this gesture, a hopeful twinge, which struck Janie in her gown and smeared face as a version of herself from the outside world, the stranger world, and communicated her worth in a way she might never have known without him. And though he couldn't have meant so much in the one part of his gesture that was public, in the private part he was trying to communicate to her that she *was* a pretty lady and she *would* be touched and that all the happiness she desired would be hers in time, if only she could bear to wait a little, to forgive herself a bit more, and to answer, when it came again, the fierce, sweet alarm of love.

SUMMER, AS IN LOVE

I WANT TO SAY that it was high summer. I want to say that
the hydrangeas were exploding, and that I was in love.
None of these things was true, exactly. It was nearly August
and the hydrangeas were tailing off, brown veins seeping in
at the edge of the purple clusters.

But, you see, this was one of those perfect summer days,
the kind that burns off all the inconvenient truths, and I
was in Vermont with my new lover, Lil Thorn, and we had
risen hot with sleep, slippery in the rude places, desperate
to start rutting again.

Oh how we rutted!

Rutted and gasped and tried not to breathe our rotten
breath onto one another. And then, toward nine, Lil shambled to the kitchen, with her big lovely strawberry of an ass
bouncing after her, and fetched us some juice and we
gulped that down and let the fructose rev our blood and
licked each other until our skin turned ticklish.

It was summer, our first summer, our only summer, and

the grass was the color of straw and the oaks on the hilltops wore skirts of black shadow and the lake down below us was an absurd milky blue. Eons ago, a glacier had passed through the surrounding valley, dug out an alluvial trough, which filled with runoff from the winter snows. The water was warm for one month a year, and we were in the thick of that month, lodged in the house of a friend who had left us his key with a note instructing us not to stain any of the furniture.

That was about our only agenda: don't stain the furniture.

We were students of literature that summer, Lil and I, and we'd brought more books than clothing. Summer was the time to catch up on the reading lists. Our duffels were crammed with Stendhal and Gaskell and James. There was always some book we should have been reading, though we were in the thick of our inaugural lust, bulletproof and glowing with sun, streaked in tanning lotion and dried sweat.

We were still reading for ideas back then, for style. We hadn't figured out what literature was for, actually, that it was mostly about loss, that without hope there was no risk and without risk there was no danger and that every story, in the end, is about danger. We still believed literature could be reasoned with, I mean.

. . .

LIL LOOKED LIKE this: tall, fleshy, with crooked teeth and a gently scalloped underlip. She'd found me somewhere, at some party, and showed me her tattoo. I was certainly ready for a major disruption.

Lil was just back from a year in Sierra Leone, doing relief work. She had the serenity characteristic of someone who has pushed past her surface fears, and this terrified and thrilled me, as did her decadence, her tendency to gorge on the sensual pleasures. The books could wait.

By noon, we had staggered down to the lake, down the steep rickety wooden stairs that led to the dock, with its quaint boathouse, where, of course, we had done it the previous day, Lil atop a bed of orange life preservers, the scent of rotting beams and boat fuel drifting down onto our sweet salty merger and the spiderwebs rising like faint scarves with our exertions.

There was a wooden float a hundred yards out, and we swam out there, with books held over our heads, *Gatsby* for me and *The Lover* for Lil. She was insatiable after doomed love, though she said she read Duras because she liked the way the author shaped her thoughts. I was stuck on Daisy Buchanan, winsome and cruel, gazing tearfully down at Gatsby's shirts (all those lovely silk collars).

We lay on our backs and held the books up to shade our eyes. And we might have gazed at the pages, absorbed a paragraph or two, but that was it. One of us would shift our weight and the raft would sway and the other would reach out. We could feel the erotic intent, transmitted through the fingertips, and the books would fall away.

In the afternoon, famished, dizzy, we drove to the country store and bought smoked ham and rolls and chocolate bars, and Brie cheese, which we slathered onto a frozen pizza. Then we curled up and slept for a few hours and rose in time to watch the shadows of the trees drawn across the lake.

Lil wanted to swim. She ran down the stairs in shorts and one of my long sleeve shirts. I might have noted her precarious gait, the way she nearly stumbled on each step. But her tits were in an uproar, swirling all around; a little clumsiness didn't strike me as any problem.

She landed on the dock, almost drunkenly, and pulled the shirt off and kicked off her shorts and she was naked there for a moment, tall as a tree and solid, before leaping into the water.

There was no one watching, no one who would have said anything. It was one of *those* lakes. Folks didn't buy houses here to spy or complain, but to remove themselves from their duties to the poor.

Lil dove down and her body jackknifed. Her bottom broke the surface for a blessed moment. She stayed under for a minute at least, then rose near the shore with her hair dripping onto her chest. Oh that chest! That water! Those pale swollen hips, which shone against her sunburn.

I was astounded at my good fortune, mistrustful, unsure what I'd done to deserve Lil. I thought surely I would be the one who made too much of our affair, forget that it was summer, just a summer thing.

AND THEN DUSK fell around us and we were into the wine, deep into the wine, two Chiantis straight from the bottle and thick as blood. It was a kind of greed that Lil made essential. Perhaps she knew what was happening inside her, that certain crucial circuits were, even then, fizzing out.

What I remember, though, is the sunlight lancing down from the stubbled brown ridges, falling across Lil as she fell against the railing of the stairs. And down below the lake, burnished in gold, the color of nostalgia—I can see that now—though at the time it was only a dappled backdrop for our next sex act.

Lil took a sip of wine and her hands were trembling and she reached back to sweep up her fine mess of black hair, to show me the delicate blue butterfly tattooed on the nape of her neck, and to lift her breasts to my caress. She stumbled a little, her knees buckled; I thought it must have been the wine, the sun, our long day of ardor.

She was wearing my shirt again (it was one of my father's old shirts, actually) and she reached down to undo the buttons and her hands were still trembling. She wanted to undress for me, there against the rail, and her fingertips played at the top button. She tried to coax the button through the hole, once, twice, three times. I thought she was being coy, prolonging the act. But then suddenly she was in tears and I said, What is it? What is it, sweetie? and she shook her head and said, No, nothing, nothing, I'm just so happy, and tried, once again, to fumble the button through the tiny stitched hole.

I reached out to help her, but she pushed my hands away and her eyes, for just a second, flashed. Let me do it, she said. I can do it.

She laughed a little, tried to laugh, but then she was weeping again, more quietly now, and I thought of Daisy, bent in obeisance over those helpless shirts, and how happy it made men to see a woman, a beautiful woman in particular, weep.

And just a little later, when we'd managed to rid ourselves of clothes, she clung to me until we were both choked of air, though when I asked her what it was all about she only shook her wild hair and bit my neck.

I COULDN'T HAVE KNOWN. She was a beautiful young woman after all, big and pink and vital. And it was summer. You don't think about such things in summer. You're in love; you think you're in love.

And then summer ends and the chilly breath of autumn

comes out of the East and the flags of skin get folded into sweaters and it gets worse, the shaky hands, the stumbling, the mood swings, until finally, just before Christmas, she names the thing and it's some disease you've seen on posters, some breakdown in the muscles—one of your teachers in junior high had the same thing, Ms. Rolff, and you can still remember the way her head shook at the chalkboard, and you, teasing her behind her back.

Who was it who pulled away from whom? I still can't keep it straight. There weren't any scenes, any blowups. We simply agreed to let the affair run down. She made it easy for me. No talk of loyalty, duty, the things I might have done.

It was only that one day I couldn't rid myself of, the golden varnish of summer, which, rather than ebbing, ebbing away as the white glare of winter took us under, grew warm and encompassing.

Lil moved on, staggered off to a new program and later, I heard, to an experimental clinic run by a doctor in Mexico. But I was still snagged in that summer idyll, the sun, the clear blue water, her skin—it was my punishment. We never think about such days as they're happening. We never consider what it means that Daisy is weeping over those shirts, feeling her betrayal before she has enacted it. We never read a book for its deepest human lesson, not in summer.

Instead, we close our eyes and let our lovers step toward us, through the fading hydrangeas, the impenetrable dusk. And when their hands tremble, we take them in ours and pledge never to leave them, not now, not ever. Even as the summer ends and the books take on their true, cruel weight, this is the story we tell ourselves, and I would trade every word in the English language for the chance, right now, once again, to believe.

LARSEN'S NOVEL

LARSEN HAD WRITTEN a novel, and his best friend, Flem Owens, had no earthly idea what to do about it. He could, in point of fact, barely lift the thing.

"What is that?" his wife, Beth, said. "Is that a rabbit? Did he give you a rabbit?"

Flem dropped the red velour binder onto an end table. This happened every time he brought home something unexpected: Beth accused him of harboring an inconvenient pet. All because, years ago, he rescued an opossum he had somewhat accidentally hit with his car and attempted—alright, he could see this now, *foolishly*—to revive the animal on their kitchen table. "Is a rabbit twenty pounds?" Flem said. "Is a rabbit made of paper?"

Beth flipped the binder open and inspected the pompous font of the title page. "So this was the big surprise, huh? Wow."

"Six hundred and seventy-three pages of wow," Flem said.

"You didn't tell me he was writing a book."

"I didn't *know.*" Flem shook his head.

He heard his daughter, Belle, pounding down the stairs in that vehement way she and her friends had. *The running of the Belles,* Beth called it.

"Did Dad get me a rabbit?" she hollered. "I heard you guys talking about a rabbit."

"No such luck," Flem said.

"What's that?" Belle began rubbing the red velour. She was eleven years old and in a rubbing phase, which unsettled Flem.

"Daddy's friend Teddy wrote a book."

Belle wrinkled her nose, a bit like a rabbit. "Why's it in a photo album?"

LARSEN LIVED IN an Eichler with his wife, Poor Jude. Flem could not think of her as anything but Poor Jude. She was a small woman with the hacked nose of a minor league hockey player and incongruously plump, firm-seeming breasts. These were her marquee feature, these breasts. Once, at a swim party years ago, Flem had found Jude alone in the cabana and watched her unsnap her top and let it fall to the wet cement. He breathed in the mildewed bamboo and coconut oil and looked at them, sagging like old grapes.

And then there was being married to Larsen, who had

insisted on an eighteenth-century British nautical theme at their wedding (not long after the swim party), because he had been on a Horatio Hornblower jag at the time. When the minister said, "Do you, Theodore . . ." Larsen shot the crowd a big grin and yelled, "Aye aye, Cap'n!" It was the sort of gesture another man—a man, say, with charm— could have pulled off. Poor Jude.

She answered the door looking, as she often did, like someone was yanking at the corners of her mouth.

"What's that smell?" Flem said. "Is that sap?"

"Incense." Jude made a befuddled noise. "Go on back. He's waiting for you."

Larsen was on the living room rug, wedged improbably into the lotus position. He had one of those exaggerated faces, the features large and set too close together. His lips and nose seemed to yearn for one another, as if he might kiss himself at any moment. He looked like a gargoyle was the truth, in the autumn dim.

"What's the deal?" Flem said. For nearly a month, Larsen had been bugging him about this meeting, saying things like *brace yourself* and *make sure you come alone.*

Larsen was trying extremely hard to appear beatific, as if he had looked the word up in the dictionary. "Sometimes in life, we reach a kind of a crossroad," he said. Larsen was a year older than Flem, and prone to weighty declarations. "A place where we realize there is more than just one person inside of us. We think there's just one person, but then we realize, uh, there's another. You see what I'm getting at?"

"I think so," Flem said. He was thinking about the Rams, who were scheduled to get clobbered by the 49ers at four.

"Put it this way," Larsen said. "'When one door shuts, another opens.' You know who said that? Cervantes, the man who wrote *Don Quixote*, which is considered perhaps the first great novel ever written."

"I think it's Cer-van-*tes*," Flem said. "Three syllables."

"Right," Larsen said. "What it is, the point, is change. Evolution. Creative growth. If you'll just close your eyes." Larsen called out to Jude, who did not respond. "Okay," he said, "just wait here. Eyes closed." Flem heard a bang, followed by a crash, followed by some nifty cursing. Larsen lumbered back into the room and placed what felt like a huge, furry music box on Flem's lap. "I wanted you to be the first one to read it," he said, "after Jude."

Flem stared at the title page. *Just Call Me Bones: A Novel by Theodore Habadash Larsen.* "Wow. I mean, since when . . ."

Larsen was grinning ridiculously. "I don't want to say too much. Because the truth is, this is just a working draft."

"But I'm not a critic," Flem said gently. "Shouldn't you show this to someone in the field? Like a professional?"

"That's the whole point," Larsen said. "I want this first novel to be the sort of work that appeals to all audiences, even the kind who consider soup labels high literature."

Flem didn't consider soup labels high literature, though he did spend more time than he would have liked to admit reading the labeling on food.

"What am I supposed to do exactly?"

"Just read and react. That's all I ask."

Flem nodded. He flipped through the pages in a bit of a daze. The house smelled of unwashed laundry and vanilla, and he could hear the small chaos of Larsen's sons in their bedroom. Teddy Jr., the four-year-old, was a little slow, but the older one, Jake, was sharp as a tack. He was blasting away on a TV video game and cackling.

"You want a drink?" Larsen said. "I feel like we should have a drink."

"I'd love to. Really. But I promised Beth I'd do some errands."

"One drink," he said. "Make it a Neer Beer."

As he pulled out of the driveway, Flem saw Jude watching him through the front window. The tight smile was still in place, the same expression, he thought, you sometimes see on hostages.

"It doesn't make any sense," Flem said. Or actually, whined. The manuscript lay on his lap, steadily pressing his quadriceps to sleep. "The guy tells me every mundane fucking detail of his mundane fucking life."

Beth shook her head. She didn't much like Larsen. Or

Jude. They were *his* friends. "Just read the thing and get it over with," she said.

This was easy for Beth to say. She tore through novels like . . . what was the expression? A bat out of hell's handbasket? Something. Flem considered himself more of a measured reader. It had taken him four years to finish the first half of that Le Carré novel, the one about the Tinker and the Sailor. He'd done better with that book about the bridges of Wisconsin, which he nearly finished before the movie came out. He'd expected to see Meryl Streep's breasts in the film and found himself angry at the book when this did not happen. "You could read it, too, honey," Flem said, snuggling Beth's elbow. "You're such a terrific reader."

"Oh no you don't," she said. "This is your fiesta, bub." She snapped off her bedside light. "I've got an off-site to handle tomorrow. Early."

This was how Beth talked since she'd become a consultant. Flem still had no idea what it all meant. He stared down at page one.

Ever since he could remember, Red Lawson had known he was different. As a baby, he had looked around the maternity ward of the hospital, at the other babies wrapped up like loaves of sterilized bread, and he had thought to himself: I am not the same. I am different.

His mother Angel and his stepfather Billy Ray had raised him to live the American Dream, and he had grown up determined to please them. He was the most handsome kid in his class, with dusky skin and bright green eyes like marbles, and the best athlete. Most of the girls had a crush on him. But Red eschewed all distractions. He even passed up the chance to go to the Olympics, even though Coach Hardy said he would have won the decathalon without even breaking a "sweat." But instead, he kept to his studies and graduated fist in his class. One day, he read a book on trends in dentistry and realized that the big money resided in the revolutionary field of gum disease prevention. His parents were so proud of him. But deep down, Red knew he was different.

He was a periodontist with the soul of a bluesman.

When Flem arrived at work the next morning, his secretary handed him a pink message slip marked URGENT.

> *From: "Red"*
> *To: My Pal Flem*
> *Message: Well???*

"He specified," Gloria said. "Three question marks."

Flem stared at his drills. "Hold my calls," he said.

By two, Larsen had called six more times. Flem phoned Beth after his 2:15, a septuagenarian with a condition Flem privately referred to as "black gum."

"Is this *Hutchins*?" Beth said. "This better damn well be Hutchins."

"It's me," Flem said.

"*Hutchins?*"

"No. *Me.*"

Beth barked something at one of her coworkers, a death threat it sounded like. "I'm tied up in an interface," she said. "Can this wait?"

"I just wanted some advice."

"Quit breathing like that. You sound like you just ran a marathon."

Gloria tapped him on the shoulder and handed him another message, this one marked MEGA URGENT.

"HE CALLS EVERY DAY," Flem told Dr. Oss. "I mean, no kidding. Every day."

"Hmmm."

"It's so self-centered. Like I don't have the rest of my life to tend to. Belle's starting to grow breasts. Beth says it's the hormones they pump into these chickens. My mother won't stick with the Saint-John's-wort. You take her out, she makes a scene. The salad bar doesn't have gherkins, whatever. And that damn dream has started up again."

Dr. Oss raised his eyebrows, his countertransference equivalent of an erection. He loved the dream—it was like a golden oldie—though it always consisted of the same thing: Flem in the middle of his life, doing something utterly routine, when suddenly no one could see him. He turned the color of his environment, the beige and whites of his office, the winter hues of Beth's decor. And life went on as usual. Occasionally someone might say, "Has anyone seen Flem?" But there was never any panic over his absence, as Flem might have preferred.

"Where were you?"

"At Larsen's."

"And?"

"I stood around."

"Might you elaborate a bit, Mr. Owens?"

"I stood around, being invisible." Flem sighed grumpily.

"I wonder," Dr. Oss said, "why you might be attracted to Larsen. If he disregards your feelings so much, I mean."

"I'm not *attracted* to him," Flem said. "He's just one of those friends, you know. We went to school together. We wound up in the same city. Our kids play. It's one of those things. You know what I mean."

"No," Dr. Oss said. "I'm afraid I don't."

THE PHONE RANG and Flem did a little involuntary neck twinge, what Beth called his "chicken peck." Belle snatched up the receiver and frowned. "Hey," she said.

From the dinner table, Flem mouthed the words: *Who is it?*

"I'm fine," Belle said, coiling the cord around her pinkie in a vaguely lewd fashion. "No. Yeah. Noooo." She giggled. "Okay. Let me check, Mr. Larsen. Okay-ay . . . *Ted*."

Flem mouthed the words, and he mouthed them very distinctly: *You don't know where Daddy is.*

But Belle, who was showing the first hints of adolescence, pretended not to see him. She held her hand over the phone and called out, "Daaaaad! Daaaaad! Pho-ooone."

Flem placed himself directly in front of his daughter: *Daddy is not here. Not here.*

Belle took her hand off the receiver and said, "One sec."

Daddy is gone, Flem mouthed, and, from the table, Beth said, "Honestly."

"Oh," Belle said, "I think that's him. He just came in."

No no no.

"Yeah, okay. Here he is."

Belle held the receiver out and Flem considered (briefly) the scene that would ensue if he punched his daughter in the mouth.

"Oh hey. Hey buddy," Flem said. "I was just out in the garage."

"You guys have a garage now?"

"Carport."

Beth made her you're-being-an-idiot sound, like a cat sneezing.

"You're a hard guy to track down. You get my messages?"

"Yeah. Didn't you get *my* messages? I left a few at your office."

"With who?"

"I don't know. Sounded like a new girl."

"I'm going to have to give her the shitcan, I swear." Larsen chuckled. "Anyway, that's a relief. I was starting to get *paranoid,* thinking maybe you were avoiding me because you didn't like the novel."

"Are you kidding?" Flem chuffed. "No way. No siree. Just busy. Super busy."

"So?"

"That's the thing."

"You haven't read it?"

"Oh no, no. I've read it. I read it all right."

Belle started to do a little tap dance, with an imaginary cane and all.

"Yeah?"

"The first couple of chapters, actually. So far."

"And?"

"I mean, hey."

"Yeah? Really?"

"Sure. I mean, strong start. Strong central character. Right there. The way you establish his difference, you know? The way he's different."

"You don't think the telepathy stuff is too much?"

"Hell no. Liked the telepathy stuff. Absolutely."

"Because I wondered if people would think, you know, it doesn't really come together until the abduction."

"The abduction. Right."

"And you don't mind that I used your name, do you?"

"Heck no."

"Because when I thought about Red's best pal, you know, it's not a strictly autobiographical novel. It's more along the lines of a magical impressionism thing. But there are some elements. Write what you know, as they say."

"Sure."

"But you like it so far?"

"Absolutely."

"You're not just saying that, right? Because, you know—" Larsen's voice deepened here, in a distressingly earnest way, "—it took me ten years to write."

"*Ten years?*"

"Probably closer to twelve. I wrote in the mornings. Before work."

"You were doing it this whole time?"

"I'd get hit with an idea just like, boom, divine instigation."

"And you didn't tell anyone."

"That was the hardest part!" Larsen's voice trilled up again. "The hardest part! But I wanted to wait until, you know, until it was done. One hundred percent."

"Right."

"So?"

"Okay."

"The rest I mean? When do you think—"

"Well now, that's a thing, a real thing. It's a long piece, a serious piece of work. And with the way things have been at the office. Boy."

"How about if you take another week?"

"I was thinking more like late December."

"December 4 it is. That's a Sunday. We'll have a little party."

"Right. I'll check my calendar. We may have a thing that weekend,"

"Hey, you're a pal, you know that? I *knew* I could count on you."

"I DON'T UNDERSTAND," Beth said. "Just read the fucking thing. Get it over with."

They had just made love, poorly. Midway through, Flem had opened his eyes and caught sight of the garish manuscript on his night table. He felt a spasm in his lumbar, his erection went south, and Beth let out a flummoxed yawn. "I can do it," he said. "You've just got to help a little." It hadn't been pretty.

"And to think," Beth said afterwards, "we once considered

filming ourselves." Now, she was sitting up in bed, stabbing at an ominous-looking chart with a Mont Blanc. "Just do a chapter a night. How bad can it be?"

Flem lugged Larsen's novel onto his chest and glared at his wife. He read aloud,

Chapter Three: In the Belly of the UFO Beast

At first, Red couldn't have said where he was. A moment earlier, he had been preparing to make love to Rosetta Stone, the most voluptuous and beautiful coed at Colgate Dental College, listening intently as she gasped at his shining manhood. But now, everything around him was like bright white crystals, as if he had been transported into one of those glass balls where you shake them and it snows.

"Where am I?" Red exclaimed in confusion.

The voice that came to him was not of this world. Yet it was the same voice that had come to him so many times before, in times of tribulation, all those times he'd thought he was just imagining things.

"Relax, Red. You will not be harmed," the voice oozed from overhead, like an ominous waterfall.

"Who are you?" Red interrogated.

"We are from the planet Galaxion," the voice boomed calmly.

"Okay," Beth said. "I get it—"

"No," Flem said. "I don't think you do."

Red tried to lift his body, thinking to make his escape. He was, after all, the state champion in the decathelon, a bona fide Olympian, according to coach Hardy. But Red found himself unable to ambulate. He was stuck in place, like a paralyzed mummy.

"Please don't attempt anything foolish, Red," the voice from above boomed. "It would be quite . . . useless."

"What . . . what do you want?" Red raged in rage.

The crystals overhead pulsed like supercharged quasars. "We want merely to guide you," the voice said. "We on Galaxion have a different conception of life than you so-called humans. We are not interested in you're 'survival of the fittest.' We are interested in maximizing the potential of all our kind. We have come to earth to observe a few select homo safiens, those of, let us say, extraordinary abilities and aptitudes. We are interested to see if they might be able to maximize their potential. With our help, of course."

"I don't understand," said Red, still confused. "But why did you take me away when I was just about to make it with Rosetta Stone?"

The voice from above chuckled in a fashion so eerie it sent shivers like tiny daggers up and down Red's muscled spine. "You would have impregnated her, had three children by her, and gone into insurance sales to support the family. By age 52, you would be dead of cancer, owing to the free-floating asbesto in your office."

"What's asbesto?"

But there was no answer from above. In fact, Red found himself back in his apartment, watching Rosetta Stone pounce back into her clothing. He remembered nothing of his experience with the Galaxions, only a vague sense of being different somehow. "Wha, what's the matter, baby?" he queried in confusion.

"I have never been so insulted in all my life," Rosetta screeched. Her green eyes blazed like a forest fire ablaze.

"What did I do?" Red declared, his eyes like the eyes of a deer whose eyes are caught in a set of headlights.

"Don't you remember? You told me I wasn't your type, and that you were sure I would meet someone someday, but that you couldn't risk your future just for the sake of a lust-based relationship."

"I said that??" Red proclaimed in confusion.

But the only answer he received was the slamming of his door, like a crack of thunder inside the eardrum of his heart.

Beth's head was under her pillow.

"Say uncle," Flem said.

"Uncle," she said.

"Proclaim it in confusion."

"'Uncle,' I proclaim in confusion."

"You're going to work with me on this?"

"Yeah," she said. "Wow. Poor Jude."

"I KEEP TRYING," Flem said. "It's right by my bedside. Top of the stack. It's just . . . I get so tired." Even discussing Larsen's novel, Flem found, made him tired. "Like a depression. Like I actually get depressed. All this stuff about the soul of a jazz musician? It's like seeing him naked." Flem had actually seen Larsen naked, about three years ago, and it had been enough to cause him to find a different gym. "You should read some of this thing. I mean it."

Dr. Oss nodded smugly. "I'm not sure that would be appropriate."

"All I'm saying is, before you make any of these generalizations about what it all *means,* you should try reading the thing."

"What do you suppose my reaction would be?"

"I think you'd understand why all the hubbub, you'd see I'm not exaggerating."

"And that's important to you? That I view this as ridiculous?" Dr. Oss scratched out a note with his fountain pen.

"Only in the sense that you'd know what I was talking about. I mean, we all have artistic impulses, okay? I took a writing class in college. But that doesn't mean that I'm going to suddenly go around proclaiming myself some kind of novelist."

"And this is what your friend has done?"

Flem shifted in his seat. He felt, as he inevitably did under Dr. Oss's simian gaze, that he was being set up. "I mean, he wrote the thing. He keeps bugging me to read it."

"Yes?"

"He's got this whole inflated sense of himself."

Dr. Oss tapped at his temple with a felty knuckle.

A chimp, Flem thought. I'm being analyzed by a chimp.

"I'm curious to know why this should occupy so much of your concern."

"Right. My concern. We're back to that." Quite unconsciously, Flem began nodding smugly.

Dr. Oss leaned forward. "You seem to be imitating me, Mr. Owens. Is that so?"

"I don't know what you're talking about," Flem said.

HE DID OWE Dr. Oss something, though, the little chiseler, because he'd discovered the answer right in his waiting room, at the back of one of the glossies he hid behind before his appointments. *Manuscripts Read,* the ad read. *Ten cents per page. Quick, professional.* He slipped one of the temps a fifty to copy Larsen's novel after hours and got it to FedEx that same night. "It's all set," he told Beth. "Done deal."

The SASE arrived the Monday after Thanksgiving. Flem

let out a whoop. "Stop being queer," said Belle. She was watching him through the railing of the stairs.

"I know you are, but what am I?" Flem yipped. Belle made a face and Flem made a face right back and skipped to his study.

Dear Mr. Larsen:

Not in thirty years as an editor have I encountered a piece of writing so egregiously misguided. In addition to your style (unremittingly cliché) and pacing (glacial), there are your characters to consider. To call them "cardboard" would be unfair, for they lacked the depth and nuance of cardboard. Your plot, if I may abuse that term, contains so many inconsistencies that two of my heartiest readers, faced with your work, were reduced to bed rest. (To cite just one: Red's mother "meets her mortal coyle [sic]" on page 36, yet appears four pages later, serving her "world famous potato salad" and looking "as diafanous as a fresh-picked daffodil.")

Just Call Me Bones is surely a labor of love, Mr. Larsen. So, too, was the Third Reich.

Sincerely,

Frederick Malyneux

P.S. Find enclosed a check for the balance of your reading fee, which I cannot, in good conscience, accept, as I only got as far as page 103.

Flem did a little dance of anguish around his study, a sort of panic-stricken fox-trot; he checked the calendar, rooted through his address book, and spent the next hour faxing an excerpt of the novel to a literary critic whose jaw he had reconstructed some years before. He received his reply, via fax, the very next day.

My Dearest Dr. Owens,

No expert, I, in this business of words (the vagaries of the literary market being something akin, from my perch, to those of Wall Street), but I believe your friend to be in possession a masterpiece. Not since Nabokov, or, perhaps, Kohlschlaunger, have I encountered a writer so deliciously attuned to the conventions of what Eagleton calls the "suburban autodidact." The wild deviations in tone, the effortless invocation of stereotype, the nearly hallucinogenic syntactical lapses. In short: wickedly, howlingly, funny.

Yet I would be remiss to leave aside the tale's unexpected rind of postmodern plangency. For so faithfully executed is Red's "story" that one feels, at odd moments, as if the author actually believes he is creating an important piece of art; it is this heartrending delusion that illumines and redeems the lacquered semiotic artifice, and redirects the reader to the garish parable itself. Beneath the farce, then, une tragedie.

The letter went on for six more pages. He glanced at the calendar above the phone. His Ansel Adams series had been replaced by a greasy, shirtless young man with what appeared to be a zucchini squash in his pants; Belle's handiwork.

"I must think," he told himself. "I must not panic."

In fact, Flem gave it no thought. "Letting the chips fall where they may," he announced to Dr. Oss. "What do you think of that?"

"What do you think I would think of that?" the little chimp bastard said.

ALL SUNDAY MORNING, the phone rang. Flem could hear his daughter, raging away like Lear outside his study. "Why can't we answer it?" she howled. "We can just lie if it's him. We've been lying for a month straight. Come *oooooon.*"

Flem rubbed his temples and, every few minutes, shouted *No!* five times, in rapid succession.

"What's his *problem*?"

"Your father is having a nervous breakdown."

"Don't tell her that," Flem snapped.

"Unplug your phone," Beth snapped back.

"He'll come over," Flem said. "I know him. I know how he *thinks.*" He burst out of his study and hurried upstairs to the bathroom, the one place where he might be able to *think.* He sat on the toilet, *thinking.* He thought about Larsen, his gummy grin, his puffy expectations. And he realized, as he sat there unproductively, that he was furious. Why should he, Ted Larsen, be the one writing a novel, when it was he, Flem Owens, who possessed the superior imagination, the *joie d'esprit,* or what have you? In a moment of excruciating clarity, he recognized that he was, of all things, *envious* of Larsen.

He made an immediate mental note to never, ever share this with Dr. Oss.

Downstairs, the phone rang. His stomach gave a yelp; his eyes settled absently on the bottle of lye, perched on the shelf above him, with its wonderful black skull and crossbones. Something like a bell struck inside his head.

This was perfect, incredibly perfect, both plausible and inviolate. Who could argue with temporary blindness? Not even a lunkhead like Larsen. He hitched up his pants and reached for the bottle, thinking that if he got the choreography just right, he could even blame Beth for this. She was the one who was so wild about lye, anyway. He didn't even know what it was for. (Termites? Mildew?) *I was just sitting there,* he heard himself saying, *when all of a sudden . . .*

Beth opened the door with the portable phone in her hand. She looked at him as he was reaching for the lye and he looked at her and in that single moment, less than a moment, an *instant,* Flem knew that his wife was on to him, had doped out the whole thing, and he felt both a deep and abiding shame and the consequent urge to throw himself down before her prostrate, or possibly supine, and further, a sense of regret that anyone, even his wife, should know him, his craven self, so thoroughly. He pondered whether his decision to adopt a policy of abject inaction in regard to Larsen's novel might have precipitated the present rather lurid scene; and, again, further, whether he might not distract Beth by throwing something at her (the lye, for instance) and then rushing past her and out the screen door.

Rather than confronting him, though, allowing him to experience his mortification and be done with it, Beth gazed at him quizzically and — in a move that stoked his long-held suspicion that she was actively collaborating with Dr. Oss — left without a word.

Now Flem wondered, annoyingly, if there was a God and more precisely how God might choose to punish him. Would it be snakes, or something with fire, or maybe having to watch the last play of the 2002 Super Bowl — the ball barely clearing the uprights, the Patriots going nuts, the Rams in agony — over and over. He sought out his wife, but found Belle standing guard outside their bedroom.

"She doesn't want to see you," Belle chirped. "You screwed up big-time. What didja do, Dad? Are you having an affair?"

Flem looked at his daughter's glossed lips and skimpy

T-shirt. The word *jailbait* flashed unpleasantly before his eyes. "Don't be silly," he said. "Your mother's just tired."

"No, she's pissed," Belle said calmly. "I told Larsen you were sick. You might want to remember that next time the whole allowance thing comes up for review."

Flem spent the rest of the afternoon puttering around the carport. He had about finished alphabetizing his tool kit when he heard Beth sigh in the doorway.

"You mad?" he said quietly.

She frowned. "Not mad so much as . . . disappointed. You're acting like an idiot, Fleming, and you're expecting Belle and me to act like idiots as well. Read the damn book and give him the snow job, or tell him you're not going to. But quit hiding. It's pathetic."

Flem certainly couldn't argue with that.

Chapter Six: Soul Daddy Bones Comes Acallin'

Red Lawson had known he was different, even before he had entered into the black maw of uncertainty that was the Galaxion's mother ship, even before he snuck out of his dorm and down to Big Willy's jukejoint and seen the black folks dance and slide to the mysterious bubbling current that flowed from the place like the scent of fatback sputtering on a potbelly stove.

The place was famous for miles around and Red could still remember his mama telling him: "Don't you go too near that place, young man. That dam of iniquity is no place for a young boy with a 166 IQ like you ." But tonight, Red couldn't help himself. He had tried to study his study cards of gingivital bacteria. But the music called out to him and washed over him like a river. And it led him out of his room and across the railroad tracks, past the hobos lounged around their snapping fires. He hesitated in front of Big Willy's, peeking through the steam-laden windows into a room roiling with black sweaty limbs that beckoned to him like serpents of temptation.

He entered the dark continent of smoke and music, and a giant bouncer type with a massive, gleaming head said, "Whobe dis little white boy?"

The music halted, and every lambent brown eye in the room fixated on him. The crowd began to ooze forward, like black lava, swallowing Red up. Suddenly, a voice rose up from the bowels beneath the room. "Dat be Daddy!" the crowd chanted, "Ooooo-yeah, man, dat be de Daddy!" The lava parted, like the Red Sea before Moses, and there stood the man known as Daddy Bones. He was dressed in a sharkskin zootsuit and a goatee clung to his chin like a small black furry animal of some kind.

"Who are you?" Red questioned.

The room boomed with laughter.

"Who he be? Eberbody know Daddy Bones!" the big bouncer bellowed. "He da most famousest black 'n blind

singer in alla East St. Louis! He like Ray Charles and Blind Lemon Johnson all wrapped in da one! Yassah!" The crowd surged forward, as if to masticate Red, but he cried out, lifting his voice until it pierced the sky above the ceiling above him: "I came to play!"

"What dat? What he say?"

"I came to play," Red proclaimed again.

"He say he come to play, he come to play!" Again, laughter cascaded around him. But Daddy Bones silenced the crowd with his finger, which was like a twig, held to his papery lips. "De boy wanna play, we let em play," Daddy Bones intoned.

Red marched toward the small raised stage, and Daddy Bones pressed the sax into his hands and Red lifted the instrument to his lips and began to blow heavenward. He felt the river of his soul swell with every color in the rainbow!

"You haven't mentioned Larsen's novel," Dr. Oss said quietly.

"No."

"Where are things?"

"Sort of a standstill, I guess."

Dr. Oss arched his chimpy little brows.

Standstill was perhaps a bit vague. The past three weekends, he had left messages on Larsen's work machine citing, respectively, an abscess conference, an allergic reaction to coconut, and a family death: all cross-checked with Belle and his secretaries.

"You've read the novel?"

"Sure."

"Yes?"

"Somewhat."

Dr. Oss pursed his lips.

"Say," Flem said, "how come you're so gaga to know about Larsen's novel all of a sudden? Who put the fire in your little red engine?"

Dr. Oss set down his pad and looked squarely at Flem. "We are here, Mr. Owens, to ask questions. For several weeks, this issue has preoccupied you. Then it disappears. I am simply asking why."

"It's like I told you, it steams me, that's all. Him going off and writing a novel and expecting me to be his cheerleading section. And then it's cruddy, and what am I supposed to do? Tell him? Which would crush the guy. Then I'm supposed to feel guilty, when he's the one who, who brought it on himself."

"Yes?"

"Sure. He didn't have to write this thing. He could have gone on like the rest of us, wiring jaws shut and battling plaque buildup. He just had to be different."

"Perhaps he's frightened," Dr. Oss said softly.

"Of what?"

"Of disappearing."

THAT NIGHT, BETH ordered Flem to stop by Home Depot for ceiling tile, and he was standing there trying to decide between cream ocher and chiffon (which looked identical to him, though to Beth the discrepancy was clearly grounds for divorce) when he heard Larsen say: "Please get down from there, Teddy. Jake, please help your brother get down." The three of them were farther up the row; Teddy had climbed into a sink display.

Flem was not frozen in place, exactly, but he felt an odd, dreamlike sharpening of his senses that seemed to recommend against movement. All around him, people were buying caulk guns and levelers and sconces, devices to brighten their lives, their hands running along edges, knocking on wood, testing consistencies. Flem watched Teddy totter into a maze of grills. "Jacob, could you please, your brother, Jake!" But Jake was into the rotisserie skewers now, waving them like a pirate. "I'm serious, Jake. Teddy, please, honey, come back. Both of you."

Jake said, "No way, loser!" and ran in the other direction, and Teddy laughed, too, and put an artificial wood chip in his mouth and something went *boom,* and this was hard for Flem to watch, because he'd supposed Larsen was having a grand old time, somehow, not struggling to keep his kids under control.

"Teddy, honey, spit that out. That's not candy!"

He felt embarrassed for Larsen, and vaguely relieved. Once Larsen saw him, he could act surprised and help corral the kids. They would have to deal with the novel, true, but then at least that would be off his conscience and into the world again. Flem said "Ted!" and "Hey!" but Larsen didn't appear to notice him. Jake shotput a brick toward his brother, which landed at Flem's feet. The boy rushed by. Larsen trundled after him, passing Flem, saying nothing.

FLEM SET ASIDE Saturday, locked his study, and cleared his desk of all but half a box of paper clips. By 3 P.M., he had constructed what he considered a passable model of the Arc de Triomphe. He napped until dinner. At half past ten, having completed chapter 7 (of 57), he slogged to bed.

"How's it going?" Beth said.

"Great," Flem said quickly. "Just great. No problems. Flying through."

"Why don't I believe you?"

"Well, yeah, I've been a little distracted."

Flem couldn't stop thinking about Larsen, there in the Home Depot, chasing after his hellions, looking out of sorts, sad. After an hour of tossing, he got up and wandered to his study. He took up the manuscript. Something in the stillness of the hour, the impossibility of other activity, helped him focus, and he found himself, if not flying through Larsen's novel, at least skittering. It was a lot like watching TV. Red bumbled from one perilous situation to the next, from Mafia back rooms to Mexican gold mines, into Massive Government Conspiracies, always somehow managing to locate a local juke joint, where he could "blow the river of his soul" through his horn. When things got too hot, Daddy Bones appeared, or the Galaxions, or sometimes both. There was a lengthy naval digression, which Flem gathered was roughly based on the *Odyssey* and which was marred by the improbable appearance of Horatio Hornblower's great-great grandson Chop. Book II was a slow-moving affair, devoted to Red's strenuous wooing of Mona Divine, the "uniquely incomparable dental hygienist of his dreams." And there were several subplots—Red's pilgrimage to the Hopi nation to treat Native American children for gum disease, most prominently—that felt both painful and extraneous.

Still, there was a certain undeniable momentum to the proceedings, once you got beyond the prose. Red wanted a lot of things and he got all of them, with little struggle. Larsen's novel was unlike life in this regard, and it lacked the tension that often accompanies life. But it was gripping in a wishful, overblown way. By the end, a cloying family scene in which Daddy Bones announces that Red is his "onliest son" (thus allowing Red to *no longer feel different*), Flem felt, if not an identification with the hero, then at least not the overt hatred that had been his initial reaction.

Outside his study, dawn was creeping in, blue and hopeful, the stars punching out. He felt an odd fondness for Larsen, and imagined him pecking away at his keyboard in the faint morning light, grinning stupidly at his metaphors, smacking his lips.

IT WAS A FINE December day, a light snow melting off and giving the world a moist, tinkly sound. He rang the doorbell three times before Teddy Jr. appeared, in his long johns. "Is your daddy here?" Teddy Jr. stumbled backwards, landed unceremoniously on a box of Cap'n Crunch, and burst into tears.

The house was in ruin: dishes underfoot, trash heaped in the sink, alps of unwashed clothes. Larsen himself was in the den, hunched over a model rocket.

"What's going on over here?" Flem said.

Larsen shrugged. He pressed the rocket's nosecone against the fuselage. Flem could see his fingertips redden under the pressure.

"I came to talk about your novel. I finished it."

"Hallelujah," Larsen muttered.

"It's good. It took me a while to get into it, which, you know, sorry about that. But I really enjoyed it. I did. The plot and all, the characters." Larsen would not look up. Flem shifted his feet. He could hear Teddy Jr. wailing away. "Where's Jude, Ted?"

"Good question," Larsen said.

"Seriously, Ted. What's going on here?"

Larsen shrugged again. "We seem to have had a rift."

"She's gone?"

Almost imperceptibly, Larsen nodded.

"Since when?"

"Wednesday? Thursday. Somewhere in there."

"What happened?"

"The book was distracting me from her and the kids," Larsen said quietly. "But there was other stuff, before that."

"God, Teddy. Why didn't you tell me?"

"You wouldn't take my calls."

Flem felt like someone had just punched him in the belly. He wished someone *would* punch him in the belly. "Christ, Teddy. I'm sorry. I've been, I really screwed up." Flem looked around Larsen's den: scattered papers, an overturned file cabinet, his prized recliner smeared with what looked like feces but was likely chocolate pudding. Teddy Jr. continued to wail. A ribbon of black smoke rose from the backyard. Was it any wonder that Larsen should imagine himself liberated from these circumstances: handsome, charismatic, soulful, somehow chosen?

"I don't guess this matters so much, but I really did enjoy the book. I'm sorry it took me so long to say so." Flem laid a hand on Larsen's shoulder, which stiffened. "I guess I was a little jealous that you'd gone ahead and written a novel."

The nosecone collapsed with a snap. "Too much pressure," Larsen whispered.

"Look, Teddy, Jude'll be back. She loves you. She probably just needs to blow off some steam. In the meantime, we should get this place in order. You know? That'd be a good place to start. Should we do that?"

Larsen stared at his hands—beautiful hands, Flem noticed. They were trembling.

The smoke in the backyard had thickened considerably.

FLEM FOUND JAKE out back, burning a pizza box on a small pyre. "The Indians burned their trash," the boy said, without looking up.

"I thought they buried it."

"Nuh-uh. Those were the Seminoles. The Plains Indians burned theirs. Big bonfires. You could see it from twelve miles away."

"Huh."

"Someone's got to do *something*," Jake said. He had

Larsen's same gargoyle face, only softened, the angles still forgiving. Flem could see a rocket launch pad set up a few paces away, the metal base blackened by exhaust fumes. "I was thinking maybe I'd help your dad get this place cleaned up a little bit. Could you maybe help out with that?"

"Teddy pooped all over the place."

"Yeah. We'll have to get him cleaned up, too."

The kid shifted his weight and glanced up at Flem through a hedge of brown hair. "My dad's a loser, isn't he?"

"What?"

"That's why you've been blowing him off. It's okay," Jake said softly. "It's cool." He grabbed another pizza box and threw it on the fire.

"Listen," Flem said. "I haven't been ignoring your dad."

"He is, though. A loser. He thinks he's some kind of writer and his best friend won't even read his book." The boy kicked at the fire. "Mom's gone, you know."

Flem felt sweat trickling from his armpits. "You're father is *not* a loser," he said. He dropped to his knees and tried to face Jake. "The reason I didn't call your father is because I didn't know what to say. I was jealous. Do you understand? What your father has done, to write a whole book, that's something amazing, something I could never do."

"Anyone can write a book that sucks."

"No," Flem said. "Not anyone can write a book. Believe

me. And your father's book doesn't suck, Jake. It's a good book. Not perfect. But nothing's perfect. Do you understand what I'm telling you? Nothing's perfect. That's not why we're here. We're here just to try. And do you know who wins, in the end, Jake? Who the winners are? The guys, like your father, who try. Those are the winners."

Jake hardened his gaze. He knew he was being lectured now, informed of those things that the adult world wished him to believe. And he knew—and Flem knew—that winners were winners and losers were losers, and trying had almost nothing to do with it. That was just something people told you, usually after you'd lost.

The boy had tuned out. Yet something in his profile, a certain intractable Larsen goofiness, buoyed Flem. Years from now, Jake, or better yet, one of Jake's children, would stumble up to the attic storeroom and find a red velour binder emblazoned with Larsen's name. And, if he were a certain sort of child, the sort willing to believe in the power of trying, he would open this binder and find inside the story of his grandfather. Not the sad loudmouth who sat cursing the Rams for their losses, but this other creature, pouring his wishes out awkwardly, unoriginally, hoping. What a beautiful thing it was, to leave your inheritors this gaudy, ill-fated record of who you were.

But that was the business of the future. For now, there

was Larsen himself, and his sons, and his wife, and the damage Flem had done all of them. He hurried toward the house, to begin cleaning. At the door, he turned and called out Jake's name and waited, full of dumb hope, for the boy to follow.

SKULL

My friend Zach stopped by for a few beers. We'd been pretty good friends in high school, gone our separate ways for college, then wound up in the same city, more or less by accident. He was a sweet guy, eager and a little sentimental at times, which probably gave us something in common. We were sitting on my couch, drinking, talking shit.

"How goes it with Sharon?" I said.

Zach sat up a little. "She's amazing."

Sharon was his new girl, a tall, elegant redhead, a little older than us. She had the kind of voice you always imagine a phone sex operator would have, moist and soothing. The unusual thing about Sharon, she had a plastic eye. Or actually, it was a polymer. Zach had clarified this for me. ("It's a polymer, man. Get it right.") She'd been shot in the eye with a BB gun when she was a kid and they hadn't been able to save it.

"We're having a great time," Zach said. "I mean, this girl knows how to have a great time."

"Lucky bastard."

"You're not going to try to work things out with Lucy?" Zach said.

I'd broken up with my girlfriend a few weeks after Zach met Sharon.

"Nothing to work out," I said.

"You guys seemed crazy about each other."

"That one night you saw us, sure. I don't know. We drove each other nuts."

"Love does that sometimes."

"I don't know," I said. "I didn't feel like I was getting to the real stuff with her."

"That's not a problem with Sharon," Zach said. He laughed a little.

"What's that mean?" I said.

"Nothing," he said.

"Nothing?"

"Not really."

He got up to fetch another beer. That was one thing about Zach. He could make himself at home pretty quickly. He settled back onto the couch and we talked about making a plan. But we were both shitty at making plans. We couldn't decide anything. The only films around were based on comic books, and we knew all the cheap bars would be full of college kids. So we kept drinking and smoked half a joint and watched the Red Sox clobber the Tigers.

"What's she up to this evening?" I said.

"Some dinner up in Auburn Hills."

Sharon did corporate fund-raising for an educational nonprofit. This explained her clothing and her sexy phone manner. It impressed me that someone could earn money attending fancy parties.

"How long has it been with you guys?"

"Nine weeks."

"Nice."

"She's special," Zach said. "There's something about her." He made an expansive gesture. He'd drunk four or five beers by now. It was hard to tell because he always put his empties in the recycling bin right away.

"Yeah," Zach said. "I lucked out."

"She's sexy," I said.

"She's sexy alright."

I let this sit. As I say, it had been a while since I'd been with a woman. "Fucking Tigers," I said. Weaver had just given up a homer to some pigeon-toed bastard from the Red Sox, I didn't know who.

"Fucking Hello Kitties," Zach said.

We didn't say anything for a while, just let the announcers drone on. I was thinking I might just call it a night, though I was worried if Zach left I'd be tempted to call Lucy up and make an idiot of myself. There'd been some of that already.

Zach got up to get another beer. He was staggering a bit upon his return.

"You okay there?"

"Sure." He sat heavily. "This is your last malt beverage. You wanna go halfsies?"

"It's yours," I said.

"Thanks man."

Zach took a gulp and swirled it around his mouth. He'd told me once that this was the best way to keep debris from settling between the teeth. His dad was a dentist, so he was full of such useful advice.

"Listen," Zach said. "You were asking about Sharon before."

"Yeah," I said.

"She's amazing."

"You mentioned that."

"There's this one thing," he said.

"What thing?"

"In terms of, like, our intimacy."

"Right."

"She likes to do different stuff."

"Different how?"

Zach glanced at the TV. It was a shaving commercial, some gorgeous idiot with the face of a Greek statue. "More offbeat, I guess. Offbeat might be a better word."

I remembered now what had always creeped me out

about Zach, which is that he had a tendency to say a little too much when he was sloshed. One night, back in college, he'd mentioned that he was sort of attracted to certain short-haired breeds of dog. "Not enough to do anything," he assured me. Still, it had pretty much killed the evening.

"She's a big fan of the face," Zach said.

"Who isn't?"

"Involving the face more."

"As in, what, like facial massages?"

"Those too," he said. He paused and glanced at the TV. "I'm going to mention something here, Pete. Okay?"

"That's the whole point," I said. "We're talking."

He glanced at the TV again.

"You want me to turn off the game?"

"If you want."

His whole posture had changed. He was sort of hunched over. I turned off the game and put on the only album we could ever agree on, which was Al Green's *Greatest Hits*. "It would have to be, like, strictly confidential. No kidding."

"Scout's honor," I said. This was an old joke. We'd both been Boy Scouts back in high school, for about two seconds.

"It's just this thing," Zach said. "This sort of sensual play, involving the face."

"Sensual play."

"She loves to feel me, you know, rubbing against various parts of her face."

"Hold up," I said. "What parts?"

"That's just it," he said. "I'm not the most experienced guy in the world, in terms of sexually. I've kind of let her take the lead."

"Yeah?"

"I don't want to freak you out," he said.

"You're not going to freak me out," I said.

What I was thinking about, oddly, was depth perception. I'd discussed the fake eye aspect with Lucy—we'd gone out to dinner with Zach and Sharon that one night—and she mentioned afterwards that she knew a girl who was blind in one eye and that it had screwed up her depth perception. This made the act of giving head difficult.

"She likes for me to rub her eye," he said.

"Her eye?"

"Not really her eye," he said. "The area around her eye."

"The socket?"

"Just listen," he said. "Okay?" He took a deep breath. "I didn't know about any of this shit, but you know she had a couple of surgeries. They've been able to make some real advances in ocular rehab." He killed the last of his beer, swished it around. "You'll notice, for example, that she can move the eye a little. It doesn't just sit there. That's because of muscles around the ocular nerves. She has to do these exercises, every night. To keep the muscles strong."

"Right."

"She does them, you know, with the prosthetic out. Most nights, I mean, by the end of the day those muscles are pretty sore. So she removes the prosthetic."

"You've watched her remove the thing?"

"No," Zach said. "She goes into the bathroom for that. Then she comes out with this patch. For the first few weeks, she always wore the patch. But this one night we'd been drinking and she asked if I wanted to see what she looked like without the prosthetic and I said yeah."

"Wow."

"It was kind of heavy," Zach said.

"What did it look like?"

"It's like, I guess, sort of like a little cup. There's some scar tissue."

"Yeah?"

"She has to rub this balm in, to keep the flesh moisturized. So this one night, a couple of weeks ago now, I rubbed the balm in for her. Does this sound creepy, man? Am I freaking you out?"

"Not really," I said.

"Because I'm not trying to freak you out."

Zach had his eyes fixed on the bouncing red lights of the

equalizer, which were rising and falling with Al Green's voice. We could hear my upstairs neighbor, dragging something heavy from one room to another.

"I could see how much it meant to her, you know, to have me accept that part of her. And the flesh there, it's extremely sensitive, the way scars can be. It was kind of a turn-on for both of us. So it just sort of evolved from that."

"Evolved?"

"Well, the first thing, she would start to touch me while I rubbed in the balm."

Zach glanced at me. His eyes were glassy with the accumulated booze; I could see now that he'd been prepping himself. "It gave her great pleasure to have me touch her there. You know, anyone can love the other parts of her. You've seen her, Pete. She's a beautiful woman. But to have a man accept that part of her, it drives her crazy. That's what we all want anyway, to have our lover accept the most damaged part of us, right? Am I right?"

"Absolutely," I said.

"So from there, it was a pretty natural progression."

"What was a natural progression?"

"That she would want me to rub myself there."

"Like a massage?"

"Sort of," he said. "But not with my hand."

"Time out," I said.

"This balm we use, it's practically like a lubricant."

"Get out of here," I said. "Get the fuck out of here."

But Zach was not the sort of guy who joked around. He lacked the imagination. And he wasn't cruel enough. That was maybe the worst thing about talking to him: everything he said was the truth.

"I didn't understand what she wanted at first. I thought she just wanted, you know, to put me in her mouth. She likes to do that. And she's excellent in that department, by the way. But then she moved. She moved down a little and she said, 'Do you trust me, baby?' I said, 'Of course I do.' It's true, Pete. I do trust her. 'I'm going to do something,' she said, and I told her whatever she wanted to do, that's what I wanted, too. So that's how it started. She took me and began to massage that area, very gently."

Zach was silent for a few seconds. Al Green was singing, *Here I am, baby, come and take me.*

"I don't want to get too technical," Zach said.

"No," I said. "You don't have to get technical."

"But to her, like I said, that's the most intimate part of her anatomy. So in that sense, what she wanted was just for the most intimate parts of our bodies to be joined, to be in contact."

"How much contact are we talking about?" I said.

"Well, at first, it was just, like, a massage. Using me to massage that area. But you have to remember, I mean, we were both naked." Zach was speaking quite softly now, fading in and out. He wasn't looking at me, thank God. He was on the other side of the couch, staring at the equalizer.

"I mean, it began as something more sensual. But at a certain point, it sort of pivoted over and there was a sexual component to it, as well. She was using her hand. She was using her mouth. I was all over the place. I couldn't always tell where I was, to be honest."

"Sure," I said.

"It's what she *wanted*," Zach said. "She wanted me to be turned on. She wanted me to get excited."

I was trying not to picture what he was talking about. But it was difficult. I kept flashing to this image of a skull and how naked all skulls look, how terribly stark and vulnerable. It was like an idea of what people really are, after all the pretty flesh has rotted away: white bone and black holes.

"The first time it was just sort of gentle like that, this gentle play. But since then, it's gotten more intense." Zach belched softly and excused himself. "There are times when I can feel she wants me to use more force. She wants me to take charge. It's not like she's issuing orders. But I can tell from the way she positions herself."

Zach glanced at me. It occurred to me he was waiting for me to say something, so he could go on.

"Wouldn't this be considered sort of dangerous?"

"Yeah," Zach said. "That's what I figured. I mean, it's a

part of the body that's been traumatized. It's right near the brain. There's all this scar tissue. That's what sort of freaked me out. I was having these fantasies of, like, something bad happening. But Sharon kept telling me, 'It's okay. I like the pressure.'" He frowned. "It's not like there's any real penetration, or what have you. The area we're talking about isn't that big. I mean, feel your eye."

I was afraid that Zach might really want me to do this, right there in front of him, but he kept talking.

"It's more like the skin rubbing against the rim, that sensitive part just below the tip, you know, rubbing, sort of up and over the rim. I don't even know what you'd call it. The thing is, Pete, it felt good. It *feels* good. Not the same as making love, but I guess it's a *way* of making love."

"Absolutely," I said.

"And Sharon, she's made it clear that she likes how it feels. She especially likes to feel me, you know, complete the act. I hope I'm not being too graphic here. Am I being too graphic?"

I paused. "It's sort of the nature of the thing," I said.

"Right," Zach said. *"Precisely."* He let out a long, beery sigh. "Anyway, it's something I've been sort of carrying around. Not like I'm ashamed. But it's just fairly intense, in terms of early relationship issues." He leaned toward me and set his hand on my arm for a second. "So thanks for listening, man."

"Of course," I said. I felt honored that he'd chosen to tell me, actually, but also a little put upon and also worried that I wouldn't be able to resist telling someone else.

"I hope this doesn't make you feel any differently about me or Sharon. I mean, I'd hate to think—"

"Not at all," I said. "What people do in the bedroom, how ever they find happiness, that's all good."

"I knew you'd understand," Zach said. He stood, a bit uncertainly, and stretched his arms out wide. "Man, I've got to piss like a racehorse."

"Sure," I said.

Zach took his leak and shambled back into the room. He said he should probably go. I could tell he wanted to see Sharon. The beers and the talk had swollen his heart.

"You okay to drive?" I said.

"Fine," he said.

"I can call you a cab."

Zach cocked his head. "No," he said. "I'll do a quick lap around the block. If I still feel drunk, I'll come back up. Promise."

Zach had survived a pretty serious car wreck in junior high and it came out later that his mom had been drinking, so I knew he wasn't bullshitting. He paused in the doorway. "Listen man, scout's honor on that stuff before, right?"

"You know it," I said.

"Cool. Cool."

I listened to him trundle down the stairs, the flap of sneakers on the damp sidewalk as he started his lap. I was kind of relieved he was gone. And then, on the other hand, I sort of missed him. The Reverend was still singing his songs, *I'm so tired of being alone,* and *Let's stay together,* all the things lovers should tell each other. It made me feel lonely, to be in possession of such a sudden intimacy. A secret can be a lonely thing to bear sometimes.

And I wouldn't have expected Zach to be the one. Of all my friends, I mean. He's not the one you'd pick out of the lineup and say, *Yeah, him, he's the one diddling his girl-friend's eye socket.*

I don't mean to cheapen the thing. It's no joke. This was something real. Sharon was a real person. Some kid, long ago, had shot her in the eye with a BB gun. And now she was carrying around this injury. She wanted her lover to touch her. There was something beautiful to the story. I could see that. But still—it left me a little shaken.

Later on, I managed to convince Lucy to come by. There was a lot of coy begging involved, though she'd had a drink or two, which helped.

It wasn't like that night was some breakthrough in our relationship. That's not the point I'm making. It just felt good to have her in my bed again, the familiar shape and heat of her. Just before we fell asleep she set her head on my chest. I could see her face in the moonlight: the round cheeks, the swell of her mouth, the shallow well of her eyes, which were wet and delicate, as precious as rare stones. Then this awful thought flashed through my mind: the worms would attack her eyes first.

I didn't want to think about it, but somewhere across town old Zach was with Sharon and they were finding their own path to love. It was—whatever, not strange or absurd, but human. Lucy closed her eyes and I let my fingers drift along her brow, her jawbone, the rim of her eyes. It was her skull I was tracing.

"That feels good," she said drowsily.

"Good."

"I'm glad you called."

"I wanted to see you."

"Keep going," she said.

"Of course," I said. "Why would I stop?"

ACKNOWLEDGMENTS

No book of short stories comes into this world without the help of many brave and foolish citizens. The following list is ridiculously partial: The entire Almond mishpochehzim, every single Algonquin book warrior, most especially Kathy, Michael, Craig, and Aimee, the various lynx-based life forms of the Bean, most prominently Erin Falkevitz, Eve Bridberg, Petey Keating, Zach Leber, Billy Giraldi, Young Bull Patterson, Timbo Huggins, Ricardo Gregg, Andrea Shea, Michelle Toth, Boris McCutcheon and his blessed Salt Licks, Web God Michael Borum, old friends and trusted rabbis Tommy Finkel, Kirkus McGurkis, Pablo Sallowpecker, and Patruchio Flood, the large body of kickass writers whose company I have been honored by and whose prose you would be foolish not to find and absorb immediately, which includes Keith Morris, Davie Blair, Chris Castellani, Jen Haigh, Redneck Machart, Karlos Roboto Iagnemma, Victor Cruzado, Juliana Baggott, Tommy Perrotta, George Skunkie Singleton, Camille Dungy, Margo Rabb, Sheri Joseph, Jim Shepard, George Saunders (and I mean that — find their books, they will cure you), the magazine folks who have allowed me to foster an illusion of relevance, most especially those at *Other Voices, Zoetrope, Missouri Review, Tin House,* and *Playboy* (the last of whom have yet to extend me an invitation to the Mansion, not that I am bitter), all of my beloved students, who remind me why I'm in the game, anyone — *I mean anyone* — who takes up the holy office of making sentences, songs, paintings, those artifacts which serve as testament to our otherwise unarticulated fears and wishes, and last but not least Abraham Lincoln, a man of astonishing eloquence and moral courage, who died, many years ago, for the sins of this country. Let us, in this age of unremitting grievance, choose as he did: to love, to sacrifice, to forgive.